The Journey Home

Children's Edition

Other Hay House Titles of Related Interest

Books

Angel Visions: *True Stories of People Who Have Seen Angels, and How You Can See Angels, Too!* by Doreen Virtue, Ph.D.

The Care and Feeding of Indigo Children, by Doreen Virtue, Ph.D.

The Dolphin: *Story of a Dream,* by Sergio Bambaren

An Indigo Celebration: *More Messages, Stories, and Insights from the Indigo Children,* by Lee Carroll and Jan Tober

The Indigo Children: *The New Kids Have Arrived,* by Lee Carroll and Jan Tober

The Journey Home: *The Story of Michael Thomas and the Seven Angels,* by Lee Carroll

The Parables of Kryon, by Lee Carroll

Card Decks

Kryon Cards: *Inspirational Sayings from the Kryon Books,* by Lee Carroll

Life Strategies for Teens, by Jay McGraw

Power Thoughts for Teens, by Louise L. Hay

✳ ✳ ✳

All of the above are available at your local bookstore,
or may be ordered through Hay House, Inc.:
(800) 654-5126 or **(760) 431-7695**
(800) 650-5115 (fax) or **(760) 431-6948 (fax)**
www.hayhouse.com

The Journey Home

Children's Edition

*The Story of Michael Thomas
and the Seven Angels*

Theresa Corley

An Adaptation for Children Ages 9 to 13
Based on the parable inspired by Kryon and written by Lee Carroll

Hay House, Inc.
Carlsbad, California • Sydney, Australia
Canada • Hong Kong • United Kingdom

Published and distributed in the United States by: Hay House, Inc., P.O. Box 5100, Carlsbad, CA 92018-5100 • (800) 654-5126 • (800) 650-5115 (fax) • www.hayhouse.com • **Published and distributed in Australia by:** Hay House Australia Pty Ltd, P.O. Box 515, Brighton-Le-Sands, NSW 2216 • *phone:* 1800 023 516 • *e-mail:* info@hayhouse.com.au • **Distributed in the United Kingdom by:** Airlift, 8 The Arena, Mollison Ave., Enfield, Middlesex, United Kingdom EN3 7NL • **Distributed in Canada by:** Raincoast, 9050 Shaughnessy St., Vancouver, B.C., Canada V6P 6E5

Editorial supervision: Jill Kramer   *Design:* Amy Rose Szalkiewicz

The author of this book doesn't dispense medical advice or prescribe the use of any technique as a form of treatment for physical or medical problems without the advice of a physician, either directly or indirectly. The intent of the author is only to offer information of a general nature to help you in your quest for emotional and spiritual well-being. In the event you use any of the information in this book for yourself, which is your constitutional right, the author and the publisher assume no responsibility for your actions.

Library of Congress Cataloging-in-Publication Data

Corley, Theresa.
 The journey home : the story of Michael Thomas and the seven angels : an adaptation for children ages 9 to 13 / Theresa Corley.
  p. cm.
Summary: An adaptation for children of the spirit writings of Kryon, who was channeled by Lee Carroll.
 ISBN 1-56170-987-5
   [1. Spiritualism—Fiction.] I. Carroll, Lee. Journey home. II. Title.
PZ7.C81625 Jo 2003
                              [Fic]—dc212002010291

ISBN 1-56170-987-5

06 05 04 03   4 3 2 1
1st printing, March 2003

Printed in the United States of America

This is for those who have learned
that a human being, no matter how small,
has the power to change his or her life and
the life of our beautiful Earth, and that
things are not always as they seem!

Contents

Who Is Kryon?

Kryon is a gentle, loving being who is with us now to help us learn about the new energy we are receiving and how to use it to make our lives better. Kryon's words have changed the way many people think and feel and have brought love and light into their hearts. The storyline for the original *The Journey Home* was inspired by Kryon and written by Lee Carroll.

* * *

Introduction

The original book, *The Journey Home,* was written by Lee Carroll, based on a story he received from a being named Kryon. On December 8, 1996, Carroll was talking to a group of more than 500 people at a seminar in Laguna Hills, California. The story he was telling, which he was receiving from Kryon, lasted over an hour and presented the journey of Michael Thomas—a man who was tired of his life on Earth, who was ready to join his spiritual family and go "Home."

The name Michael Thomas represents both the sacred and holy qualities of the Archangel Michael and the old-energy qualities of Thomas the Doubter in the Bible. This combination is like many of us who feel that we're good people, but are bashful and can't quite believe that we're as wonderful as the angels.

Michael's journey home is an adventure through seven colorful houses, each occupied by a Grand Angel. Each house represents a quality of the new energy and shows it to us as a humorous, wise lesson. We also come to understand what it is that God wants us to know about ourselves and how things work as we move through life in the new energy that's here on Earth now. The end of Michael Thomas's journey surprises us as we learn about our partner, who loves us more than anyone and helps us always.

If you have ever asked God, "What is it You want me to know?"—*this may be it!* Join Michael Thomas in his exciting journey. It may remind you of your own.

*　*　*　*　*　*

Chapter One

Michael Thomas

The black plastic pieces flew in all directions as Michael Thomas (Mike) threw the model airplane a bit too hard against the wall. He was just so tired of this junk pile that was supposed to be *his* room—even though he had to share it with his big brother. The crash must have been something, because his mom called from the kitchen to ask, "Everything okay in there?"

The room was divided in half by a long rug, so Mike could point to his part of it. But his brother always came in and out like a hurricane, leaving his dirty laundry, and model airplanes, and smelly soccer gear crammed in wall-to-wall. You couldn't even tell Mike lived there, he was so swallowed up by his brother.

Mike didn't answer his mom but muttered under his breath, "No one would miss me if I just disappeared."

But where was he going? Nowhere. It would be a long time before he'd ever have a room to himself. He didn't have the strength to clear all the mess from his side, so all he could do was stand in the middle of the heaps and sigh. A yellow smiley face looked up from a plastic cup under a dirty sock, but it couldn't cheer him up. It didn't matter how many smiling faces he saw scattered in the mess, Mike still felt stuck. What was there to smile about? His mom had noticed that he was staying sad too long and had already been asking him about it.

Mike was in Mrs. Davis's sixth-grade class, about to go into junior high and enter a whole new school. It was almost summer, and Mike felt as if he'd been going to school for a hundred years. He was so tired of taking tests and studying—he felt all that he'd learned was how to pass tests, not all the stuff a sixth-grader needed to know by now.

He didn't have time for friends and didn't want any. Bryan, his last good friend, had moved away at the beginning of the school year, and it wasn't fun to ride his bike or play baseball any-more. There was no one to really talk to. He'd never have such a good friend again.

So, Mike lived in his own little world that he shared with his goldfish. He'd wanted a dog, but his father wouldn't allow it, so he named his fish "Dog" just for fun.

He was absolutely miserable about his situation, and he knew he needed to just get over it, but he didn't know what to do about it yet. "Hang in there, Dog," Mike would say to his golden friend on his way out of the room. Of course, Dog never said any-thing in return.

The guys in his class sometimes asked him, "Mike, when are you going to get a grip? You need to get back on the team again and quit being by yourself so much. We miss you." Then they would go home to their families and friends—and some-times dogs, too. Mike went straight home from school and didn't participate in any school activities or sports—almost like he was punishing himself for his friend Bryan having moved away. But Mike couldn't understand how to shake this "lost" feeling. It wasn't worth it, he decided. He figured he'd already had the best friend he was ever going to have.

Bryan had to move because of his dad's new job. Mike and Bryan had been best friends since kindergarten, and Mike expected that they'd go all the way through high school together. But Bryan's dad just wiped that all out. It was as if Mike's entire future had shriveled up and disappeared—his secrets and plans had all moved away.

All his life, Mike had lived on the same street in his little town. The people on his street were so friendly, and they really liked and trusted him. He helped his parents and didn't run around making a lot of noise and tearing things up. Several of his neighbors were older and needed a helping hand, so they sometimes asked him to do chores for them. His manners were great, and he did such good work that they'd pay him a little extra when the job was done. He saved all his money in a big green water bottle, which filled up in no time since he was a natural. People loved to be helped by Michael Thomas.

When he thought about Bryan and was feeling really down, Mike realized that all he had left besides his family was God. Kids don't usually spend a lot of time thinking about God, but Mike was sure that God loved him and must have just forgotten about him temporarily. A lot of good God was doing right now. Mike still went to church with his parents and prayed for Bryan to move back—but he didn't really believe that it would happen. Then he'd stare at the big stained-glass window at the end of his pew, the one with the giant golden angel, and get king-sized goose bumps when the angel looked right at him.

Mike had a lot of heart. He opened doors for people at the market and spoke courteously to his elders. It bothered him when people just walked right by each other without speaking. He felt that everyone should be friendlier and work together to make things better. That's how he'd been with Bryan. Mike knew that things were going to be much better for Bryan's family with the new job, but Mike still didn't see why he had to lose his friend. He felt nothing should be more important than friendship.

✳   ✳   ✳

And so it is that our story really begins. Here was Michael Thomas at his saddest, making his way home on a Friday afternoon after a rough day at school, to a room that was buried somewhere under smelly soccer clothes. He'd stopped to take Mrs. Burns's groceries into her house, earning a dollar for his help. It always surprised him how easy it was to make money when all he was trying to do was help. And he hardly spent any of it. Who would he spend it with? Mike didn't go anywhere—he only read and thought in his room.

A heavy mist was still trying to turn into rain when he left Mrs. Burns, making the streetlights come on in the early darkness so that everything looked slick and shiny. Since Bryan had left, Mike would ask his mom why they didn't move to a place where the weather wasn't so wild. She'd just smile and say, "Families stay where their roots are, you know. Besides, it's safe here." She thought that other cities were dangerous. Mike tried to tell her that there were bound to be other towns as nice as theirs, but she just wouldn't hear it.

Mike made up his mind to leave as soon as he finished school. He'd be old enough then, so he'd find Bryan and live in *his* town. He wished they'd been able to spend more time together before his friend moved.

In the dim light, Mike trudged down the sidewalk toward home. He turned to see that Patch was following him again. Patch was Mrs. Burns's dog, an old friend who followed him home from school almost every day. Mike knelt down to give him a quick hug and buried his face in Patch's soft fur, so he didn't see the car when it came squealing around the corner and hit the slick spot in the road. He didn't see the wheels lose their grip on the road where it was so slippery from the mist. When the car hit him, he didn't see anything at all. Everything went black.

The minutes flew by in a flash. Mike didn't understand what had just happened to him, and it was still dark, so he started to panic. He couldn't move in the darkness, either, and that sure didn't help the situation any. The noise was just terrible.

The pain was bad, and Mike couldn't breathe. He coughed and choked, trying to make some air go into his lungs. Patch was barking and licking his face, trying to get his friend back up on his feet. Mike's back and legs felt as if they were on fire, and he couldn't understand why there was so much noise. An ambulance siren wailed as it came closer, and he could hear Mrs. Burns yelling at someone, "What's happened? Is the boy all right?" Then it was quiet.

✳   ✳   ✳   ✳   ✳   ✳

Chapter Two
The Vision

Mike woke up in a strange place. It was so quiet that it made him uneasy. He could hear his own breathing! No passing cars, no barking Patch, no wailing siren. He sat up a little.

Mike looked around and saw that he was lying on a narrow white bed. There were no covers, and he was still wearing what he'd had on at the time he heard the car tires screeching. He reached down and touched his legs. They'd burned so much earlier that he thought they must have really gotten hurt. But to his relief, they weren't. He actually felt good! He gently poked himself in a few places. It was weird, but there was no injury or soreness at all.

But the silence! After all that noise on the street, it sure was strange that he couldn't hear anything here. The light was different, too. It was so bright, but he couldn't tell where it was coming from—it almost hurt his eyes. He looked around, squinting to check things out.

It was spooky. Mike wasn't in a room—and he wasn't outside! The white floor stretched for as far as he could see. He lay back down. He knew what had happened. The car had killed him. It didn't take a rocket scientist to understand that what he was seeing and feeling didn't make sense in the real world. But why did he still have his body?

Mike pinched himself to make sure he wasn't dreaming. He flinched and uttered a loud "Ow!"

"How do you feel, Mike?" asked a soothing male voice.

Mike looked quickly in the direction of the voice and saw a sight he would never forget: a figure in white who was more beautiful than anything Mike had ever seen. *Are those wings? It looks just like the angel in the window at church!* Mike stared at the vision in front of him in disbelief.

"Am I dead?" Mike asked in as manly a voice as he could, but with respect for the being before him.

"Not at all," said the giant angel, who slowly moved through the light. "It's a dream, Michael Thomas." The beautiful ghostly figure floated closer until he was at the foot of the bed. Because the room was so bright, Mike couldn't see the being's face clearly. But the soothing sound of the figure's voice and the warm, sparkling light made Mike feel comforted, safe, and cared for.

The angel's garment seemed somehow alive, and it moved with him as though it were his skin. There weren't any folds, buttons, or creases where clothing ended and skin began; yet the odd robe wasn't tight—it was silky and flowing. The angel's whole body seemed like it was glowing and blurry.

"Where am I?" Mike asked in a very small voice.

"You're in a sacred place. A place you made, which is filled with great love. That is what you are feeling right now."

The angelic figure bowed to Mike, and the light in the room got even brighter.

"Who are you?" Mike asked respectfully, his voice shaking a little.

"I am an angel, as you have already guessed."

Mike didn't blink an eye. He knew that the vision in front of him was telling the absolute truth. The situation was stranger than any Mike could have ever imagined. And yet somehow, he knew it was real.

"Are all angels men?" Mike was sorry he'd asked the question as soon as it left his lips. *What a dumb thing to ask!* This was obviously a very special time. Mike didn't want to waste it. What if it was just a dream, and he woke up and it was over?

"I am only what you wish to see, Michael Thomas. I don't have a human body, so you see me in this way so that you won't be afraid. But no—all angels are not men. We are not men or women. We do not all have wings either."

Mike smiled. It began to feel a bit easier to speak to this gentle being. "What do you really look like? And why can't I see your face better?"

"My shape would amaze you, and at the same time you would feel as if you had seen it before because it is the way *you* look, so I will continue to look like this for now. As for my face, you will see it soon enough."

"When I'm not on Earth?"

"Earth life lasts only a short time, but you know that. I know who you are, Michael Thomas. You are a young man who knows God, and you understand that people live long in God. We have heard every word each of the many times you have spoken to God and thanked Him for things He has done for you."

Mike was silent. Yes, he'd prayed in church and at home, talking to God like He was sitting right next to him, but to think that this angel had actually heard him?

"Where do you come from?" Mike asked.

"Home." The loving being tilted his head to the side patiently while Mike tried to understand.

Mike felt tingles go up and down his back. He had the sense that there was great truth standing here before him and that he had only to ask and wonderful knowledge would pour out.

"You are right!" The angel responded to Mike's inner thoughts. "What you do right now will change your life. You are feeling it, aren't you?"

"You know my thoughts?" Mike was a bit embarrassed.

"No. We can *feel* them. Your heart is connected to all of us, you know, and we answer when you need us."

"We?" Mike looked around again. "I can only see you."

The angel laughed, and the sound was exciting to hear. What energy that laughter had! Mike felt every cell in his body fill up with the sound of the angel's laughter. Everything the angel did was fresh, larger than life, and somehow stirred a wonderful memory of something deep inside him.

"I speak to you with my voice, but I speak for many." The angel held out his arms, letting his odd robe roll like a wave on the ocean as he moved. "There are many angels to help each human, Michael. You will see this if you choose to let yourself do so."

"I *do* choose!" How could an invitation like that be ignored? Mike stayed quiet and watched the angel move gently up and down, just barely floating, like his robe. He thought again that this might be his imagination—too many movies? Staring too long at the angel window in church?

It seemed that the angel wasn't going to say anything more unless Mike asked more questions. "Is it okay for me to ask about what's happening to me? Is this really a dream? It seems so real."

"What is a human dream, Michael Thomas?" The angel moved slightly closer. "It is a visit into your mind and your heart that helps you to receive information from my side of things—sometimes like a story. Did you know that? The way things happen in dreams is closer to the way things actually are in Spirit.

"Those times that you dreamed about Bryan, after he moved away—how did that make you feel? It was like being with him again, wasn't it? You walked around with your head down for days because you were so sad when you woke up. The dreams were real. He keeps thinking about you, too, Michael, because your friendship was strong. The power of that friendship will stay with you both even though you are not together. Why do you think you are having this dream now? Because of the way your life was going—it was time for it to happen."

Mike was comforted by the long stream of conversation from this beautiful one, who seemed more and more familiar to him. It was as if Mike knew him from somewhere. "Will I come out of this okay? I was badly hurt before I came here, and I think I'm passed out somewhere, maybe dying."

"That depends."

"On what?" Mike didn't know what to think.

"What is it you *really* want? Be careful with your answer, Michael Thomas, for the energy of God works exactly as you ask. Besides, we know what you know. You cannot fool your deeper self."

Mike did remember dreams about Bryan that seemed like they really happened. They'd hung out and joked around just like old times. In one dream, Bryan even told him that he *had* to move, that it was time for Mike to move on to other friends . . . it was a gift, it was part of the arrangement. What kind of gift was losing your best friend? What kind of arrangement? That dream had really upset Mike, and he couldn't make himself believe anything other than that Bryan's leaving was the end of his life.

But then again, it was only a dream . . . or was it? The angel said it was real. Being here certainly seemed real, so maybe Bryan's messages were, too. This was confusing and disturbing to Mike. He thought about his life and all the things that had happened to him in the past year. He thought about going to a new school where he had no friends. He thought about sharing a locker with a stranger who might steal his lunch. He thought about his brother, who seemed to forget that they were supposed to be *sharing* a room. He knew what he really wanted, but he felt it was wrong to ask for it.

"It is not worthy of you to hold back your innermost desires—you are too magnificent for that," the angel gently told Mike.

Gee! The angel still knows what I'm thinking. I can't hide a thing! Mike thought. Out loud, he said, "If you already know, then why are you asking me? And what's this *worthy* stuff? And why do you say I'm magnificent?"

"You have no idea what and who you are, Michael Thomas. You think *I* am beautiful? You should see what *you* look like. Someday you will. As for my knowing your thoughts and feelings, of course I do. I am here as one of your helpers, so I am with you all the time. It is my honor to appear before you, but it is your intent—your purpose—that will change things now. You have the choice to tell me—or not to tell me—what it is you want most right now as a human. The answer has to come from your own heart, spoken out loud for all to hear—even for *you* to hear. What you do at this point will make a difference for many."

Mike thought about it. He'd have to speak his truth even though it might not be what the angel wanted to hear. He thought for a minute, remembering where the angel came from, and then spoke.

"I want to go HOME! I'm tired of my life so far as a human, and I want to go where *you* come from." There! He'd said it. He wanted out. "But I don't want to mess up something important to God's plan." Mike was serious. "I feel stuck and alone in my life . . . but I know that I was created in the image of God for a purpose. What can I do?"

The angel moved to the side of the bed so that Mike could see him better. It was amazing, this vision, dream, or whatever it was. Mike swore he could smell flowers. Why? The angel actually had a smell! It—he—was more beautiful the closer he got. Mike was also aware that the angel was pleased with their discussion and his thoughts. He could feel it, even though he couldn't tell what the look was on the angel's face.

"Tell me, Michael Thomas: Is your intent pure? Do you really want what God wants? You want to go Home, but you also understand that there is a greater plan—so you do not wish to disappoint us, or do something that is not spiritually proper?"

"Yes, that's it exactly. I'm not happy with my life anymore, and I want to leave it, but I feel like I'm being selfish if I don't stick it out."

"What if I told you that you might be able to have both?" The angel smiled. "You will not disappoint us. Your wish for Home is natural, not selfish. And you will still be able to do what you came here to do."

"How? Please tell me how I can do this." Mike sat up straight.

The angel had seen Mike's heart, and now he honored him spiritually for the first time. "Michael Thomas of Pure Intent, so that we may know if you will be allowed to go Home, I must ask you one more question before I tell you any more." The angel moved away slightly. "What is it that you expect to gain by going Home?"

Mike gave this some thought. The angel understood why it was taking him so long to give his answer, knowing that this was a sacred time for the soul of Michael Thomas. Several minutes passed, but the angel never moved or said a word. He was in no hurry. Mike was beginning to understand that time didn't mean the same thing to angels as it did to humans.

"I want to be loved and to be around love," was Mike's answer. "I don't want to be so sad and lonely anymore. I want to know that everything will turn out all right, and that I'll be able to do what I'm supposed to do in my life. I don't want to be like *me* anymore, I want to be like *you*. That's what going Home means to me."

The angel moved to the foot of the bed again. "Then, Michael Thomas of Pure Intent, you shall indeed go Home!" It didn't seem possible, but the angel appeared to get brighter! He absolutely glowed white, and then became gold. "But you must follow a certain path, and it must be your choice and intent to do so. You will then be rewarded with a trip Home. Will you do this?"

"I will." Mike felt the beginnings of a wonderful feeling that could only be described as a wash of love. The air was starting to feel thick. The glow of the angel was starting to creep into the bed and around Mike's feet. Chills began to go up his spine, and he began to feel a strange, fast vibration. It traveled up his body and into his head. He started seeing flashes of blue and violet against all the bright white he'd been looking at since all this started.

"What's happening?" he asked fearfully.

"Your intent is changing everything."

"I don't understand." Mike was scared.

"I know. Do not be afraid, because you are just feeling more of God's love in your body. It is part of what you asked for, and it will help you on your journey Home." The angel backed away from Mike's narrow bed as if to give him some room.

"Please don't leave yet!" Mike still didn't understand every-thing that was happening to him yet, and he was afraid.

"I am just changing my position to handle your new size."

The angel laughed as he explained. "I will leave only when we are complete."

"I still don't understand, but I'm not afraid anymore," Mike lied.

Again the angel laughed and filled the air with a vibration that surprised Mike. The vibration seemed full of wonderful happiness and powerful love.

Mike knew that the angel would know his thoughts any-way, so he continued to speak. He had to know what this feel-ing was. Then the angel laughed again. "What is it that hap-pens when you laugh? It gives me a tingle inside, like nothing I've ever felt before."

The angel was pleased by the question. "What you hear and feel is something that comes only from God. Humor is one of the few things that doesn't change when it goes from our side to your side. Did you ever wonder why only humans laugh, and not dogs or cats or trees? You might think that the animals laugh, but they truly do not. A dog does not sit down and remember how a cat got splashed in a puddle the other day, and then laugh at how funny its droopy, dripping whiskers looked. Only humans do that. There is a spark of God in humans that allows them to think of things that are funny. This is the key. Believe me, it is sacred. That is why it helps people so much, Michael Thomas of Pure Intent."

Mike realized that he had many questions he wanted the angel to answer. He decided to jump right in and ask, "What's your name?"

"I don't have one." There was the silence again. A long pause.

Well, Mike thought, *we're back to short answers.* "What do they call you?"

"I AM known by all, Michael Thomas—and THAT I AM known by all; therefore, I exist."

Mike didn't have a clue what that meant and could only say, "I don't understand."

"I know." Again, Mike could make out that the angel had a little smile on his face.

Mike knew that the angel's smile wasn't because he thought Mike was stupid. The angel knew that Mike just didn't understand yet. There was love in everything the angel did and said.

Mike decided he'd better get to the point. "What is the path you're talking about, dear angel?" It sounded strange to call the angel "dear," but it felt right. The angel was like a mom or dad, but felt like a best friend, too. He wanted to stay in this energy forever, and he dreaded the thought of leaving.

"When you go back to your old life, Michael, get your things together for an adventure that will last for several days. When you are ready, the first step of the path will be shown to you. You will visit seven houses of Spirit, and in each house, you will meet an angel like me, each with a different job. There will be some surprises, and there may be some danger along the way, but you can stop anytime you wish. On this adventure, you will learn the ways of Spirit. If you stay on the path and visit all seven houses, then you will be shown the door that leads to Home. And Michael," the angel paused and smiled, "there will be great celebration when you open that door."

Mike had no idea what to say. He was excited, but also pretty nervous about not knowing much about the path and the houses. What would he find? Should he do this? Maybe this was just nonsense! How did he know that the angel was real, anyway?

"What you have here is real, Michael Thomas of Pure Intent," said the angel, again reading Mike's feelings. "What you will go back to is a life that was only arranged to help you learn, like acting in a school play."

Mike didn't like his thoughts known, yet he felt honored that they were important to the angel. *In a dream,* Michael thought, *I know what's in my own brain, so I don't have secrets from myself. And since this angel is my helper, and always with me, it makes sense that there would be no secrets from him either, and it's okay.* Mike was beginning to feel very comfortable in this dream life, just as the angel had said he would. He didn't want to go back to the loneliness of his old life.

"What now?" asked Mike slowly.

"You have given intent, choosing to take the journey. So you will return to your life. There are some important things to remember along the way, though. Things will not always be as they seem, Michael. As you go, your world will change to be more like mine, so you must learn a new way to think." The angel paused. "You will have to think more about things as they are happening NOW."

Mike didn't understand this at all, but listened closely anyway.

"There is another question that I have to ask you now, Michael."

"I'm ready." Mike was feeling a bit unsure of himself, but was honestly ready to get started. "What's the question?"

The angel moved right up to the edge of Mike's bed. "Michael Thomas of Pure Intent, do you love God?"

Mike was surprised at the question. *Of course I do,* he thought. *Why did the angel ask?*

Quickly, he replied, "Since you can see my heart and know my feelings, you must know that I love God." There was silence, and Mike could tell that the angel was pleased.

"Indeed!" It was the last word that Mike heard from this beautiful creature who obviously loved him very much. The angel reached out and moved his hand over Mike's stomach and legs. Immediately, Mike felt as if hundreds of fireflies had flown into his body and were changing him. It didn't hurt, but suddenly, he threw up.

* * * * * *

Chapter Three
Preparation

"Hold his head to the left, next to the tray!" cried the nurse to the orderly. "He's vomiting!"

The emergency room was crowded that night, as it was almost every Friday night. There was a full moon, too, which usually made things worse. Most people think it's just an old folk tale that the full moon has a strong effect on us, causing more accidents and crazy situations than at other times. But just the same, many hospitals make sure that there are plenty of doctors and nurses in the emergency room on those nights.

The nurse looked down at her beeping pager and rushed out of the room to take care of another sick person.

"Is he awake?" asked Mike's mom.

The white-coated orderly bent down to take a closer look into Mike's eyes. "Yes, he's coming out of it. But don't let him get up— he's pretty banged up, and he's going to be very sore for some time."

The orderly left the room, closing the curtain so that Mike and his mom were alone again. The emergency room was noisy all around them. Lots of people, lots of pain. Many of them had been there almost as long as Mike had—about an hour and a half.

Mike opened his eyes and felt a terrible burning sensation in his leg. Boy, was he awake! *No more angel dreams,* he thought, as the pain brought him rudely back to his world. The light in the room was much too bright, and the room was too cold . . . he closed his eyes and wished he had a blanket.

"You've been out for a while, honey," said his mom. "They got you all fixed up, though. Don't try to talk."

Mike looked at his mom, feeling so much love for her. He was lucky to have her. She put her hand on his forehead, and he fell back into a very deep sleep.

* * *

When Mike woke up again, it was still and quiet around his bed. He opened his eyes and looked around, realizing that he was in a room by himself. And what a room! The ceiling had beautiful designs on it, and the lights were soft. Most of the light, though, was coming from a big window. And the furniture was really nice. There was a beautiful lamp, and its shade matched the wallpaper! *What kind of place is this? Some fancy hotel?* Mike wondered in amazement.

Then he spotted the big plugs and switches on the wall and the same equipment he'd seen in the emergency room earlier. A machine attached to his arm by some clear tape beeped softly every few minutes. It was a hospital—but not like any hospital Mike had ever seen before.

There seemed to be no one around. Mike tried to figure out what was going on—what in the world had happened? Did

they operate on him? Could he move his legs? Slowly, he felt around his stomach, almost scared by what he might find. No bandages, no cuts! He sat up a bit to feel around on his legs and found nothing there, either! He knew he'd been hurt, so why weren't there bandages? Was he dreaming again?

Mike poked around a bit more on his stomach. Stinging red pain, enough to make him sick, instantly stabbed Mike down deep inside. *I guess I'm not dreaming,* he thought, as he decided not to poke around or move much anymore.

"Oh, we're awake I see. We can give you something for the pain, Mr. Thomas," said a whining but kindly lady's voice from the door. "But you'll get better faster if you stay still. Nothing's broken, you know." The nurse came up to the bed. Her uniform was fancy and fresh with no wrinkles, and from all the award pins and service badges above her pocket, Mike could tell she was a good nurse.

Mike spoke carefully, trying not to move as he talked. "Where am I?" he mumbled.

"You're in a private hospital, Mr. Thomas." The nurse moved next to him. "You spent the night here after they brought you over from the emergency room. You'll be leaving shortly." Mike's eyes opened wide, and his face wrinkled with worry. He knew that it must cost a bundle to stay in a beautiful hospital like this one. His heart began to pound as he wondered how his parents would ever be able to afford such a place.

The nurse spotted Mike's worried look. "It's okay, Mr. Thomas. Everything's been taken care of. A man came in earlier and took care of all the arrangements—it's all been paid for."

Mike was quiet for a minute, trying to think of who that man could have been, because surely his dad didn't have that kind of money.

"Did you see the man?" Mike asked. He was sure that there had been some mistake.

"See him? Oh, yes! He was very handsome. Tall and blonde, with the voice of an angel. Paid for everything in cash. Don't you worry now, Mr. Thomas. And, oh yes . . . he left a message for you."

Mike felt his heart jump. He didn't know anyone that matched the nurse's description of the man—and now there was a message for him, too?

The nurse soon returned with a piece of paper and handed it to Mike. "The gentleman said his writing wasn't very good, so he had us type this up for you. Kind of mysterious, if you ask me. It was funny, he called you *Opee.*"

Mike read the note silently to himself:

Dear Michael-Opi,

Not everything is as it seems. Your journey begins now. Get well fast and get your things ready for the journey. I have prepared the way Home. Take this gift and move forward. You will be shown the way.

Mike had goose bumps. He looked at the nurse gratefully and held the paper to his chest. Then he closed his eyes so that the nurse would know he wanted to be alone. She understood and quietly left the room.

Mike's mind raced with a zillion thoughts. *"Not everything is as it seems,"* the note said. No joke! He knew that his stomach and legs had been very hurt yesterday. Yet now there were only some bad bruises. They'd be sore for a while but wouldn't keep him in bed. Was that the gift the note spoke of?

Mike didn't really believe that the visit with the angel had actually happened until he read the note. The man who paid for everything at this fancy hospital *had* to have been the angel! No one else could have done that for him. And who else would have

known about his journey? His body was buzzing with questions. He was still in a state of shock when he remembered something.

The nurse had mentioned that the stranger called him *Opee*. On the note it was spelled "Opi," like a name. But no one Mike knew had ever called him by that nickname. All of a sudden, Mike realized that the letters were initials! *O-P-I—Of Pure Intent!* So that's what it said—*Dear Michael of Pure Intent.* Mike's smile turned into a laugh. It hurt a lot, but he couldn't quit laughing, and his whole body shook with it until tears of joy and relief flowed down his face. He was going Home to his new life!

$$* \quad * \quad *$$

The next few days were so special. Mike left the hospital with some pills that the nurse said he could take for pain, but Mike didn't need them. His bruises seemed to be healing with incredible speed. He was a bit stiff when he moved, but he could handle it, knowing that it could have been so much worse. He wondered why it wasn't.

Mike stayed home from school. The school year was almost over, but he was still glad to get a short break from it. Mrs. Burns brought Patch over to visit him in the backyard. Mike could tell that the little dog was happy that he was back home and getting well. Most of the time, Mike stayed in his room and thought about the mysterious stranger and his visit from the angel. Sometimes he'd read. His mom kept checking on him because he was quieter than usual, but she thought it was because he was still a little weak from the accident. She tried not to ask him too many questions, which was a good thing, because Mike didn't know how to tell her he was about to go away again. He believed that once he was gone, his mom would somehow find out about his journey and understand his need to leave. *Moms always know everything,* he thought.

Mike gradually started getting ready for his journey, carefully collecting what meant the most to him. What little there was fit nicely into a cigar box with a rubber band around it. He knew he wouldn't be able to carry many clothes, so he dragged his old gym bag out from under the bed and stuffed into it only a shirt, jeans, a pair of socks, and underwear. Then, he emptied his chore money from the big green water bottle into a little cloth sack his dad had given him. He hoped $47.51 would be enough money for wherever he was going. He zipped the cigar box and the money sack into the gym bag, and decided he was ready to go.

Mike thought his pet fish looked sad swimming around in the glass bowl.

"Don't worry, Dog, my mom will take good care of you while I'm gone. You just hang in there," Mike reassured him.

Five days had passed since he had come home from the hospital, and Mike felt that his journey would start any time now. It was evening, and all was quiet as he lay in his bed. He didn't know what to do next, and he didn't really know where he was going. But he was sure that the angel was watching over him.

Mike knew that tomorrow would be the start of something new. He didn't worry about the details—he was confident that he'd be shown what to do. Everything that had happened in the past week made him sure of that.

Mike decided to rethink what he'd tucked into the cigar box. Did he really need all that stuff? He got up and took the box out of his gym bag. Besides the baseball cards Bryan had left him, there were some neat old game pieces, some coins from Mexico and Germany, three clear crystals, an old family picture, and his fifth-grade class picture.

Mike picked up the photo of his class. There they were, he and Bryan smiling happily in the last row. Fifth grade had been a breeze. They had made so many plans together. . . . Mike sighed, looking at his friend in the picture.

"I guess I have to go on this adventure all by myself. I hope to see you again soon, buddy, and I'll tell you all about it then." Mike knew he couldn't leave any of this stuff behind, so he loaded his gym bag with all of his prized possessions.

Everything fit just fine in the bag, and it wasn't too heavy. He'd even be able to stuff in a snack or two. Mike lay back down on his bed for the last time. He was so excited about his journey that he almost couldn't get to sleep. He kept thinking about all that had happened in the last few days and what would happen on his journey to come. Tomorrow would be the big day!

* * * * * *

Chapter Four
The First House

The next morning dawned a bit dreary, but Mike's spirits were high. Sneaking out of the house was no sweat. He walked for a while and decided to buy himself a big breakfast with some of his chore money. He ate at a table outside the little fast-food place. It felt weird to be out and about at this time of day—usually he was at school by now, bent over an assignment.

Mike ate most of his breakfast, saving just a bit for later. He knew most of the roads around his neighborhood, but he realized that he had never gone very far from home by himself. Bag in hand, he stood and looked around. *If only I had a map that could tell me exactly where I'm going,* Mike said to himself as he started walking through the little neighborhood.

He didn't know why, but he felt he should just keep heading in the direction of the sun. At lunchtime, he sat down on a curb and ate what he'd saved from breakfast. He wondered again if he was on the right path.

"If you're there, I need you now!" Mike said out loud to the sky. "Where does my journey start?"

"A current map it shall be!" Mike heard a familiar voice speaking in his ear. He stood up and looked around but saw no one. He knew it was the angel.

"What took you so long?" Mike asked with a little laugh. He was thankful to hear from the angel again.

"You only asked for help a moment ago," answered the voice.

"But I've been walking for hours!" Mike protested.

"What took you so long to ask us for help?" The angel turned Mike's words around on him.

"You mean I only get help when I ask for it?" Mike said, frowning.

"Yes. You are a free spirit, honored and powerful. You are able to make your own way if that is your choice. You have been making choices all along. We are always here, but we help only when you ask. Is that so odd?"

The angel made sense—it was so simple. Mike was irritated with himself because he hadn't asked for help sooner.

"Okay, where do I go? It's already after noon, and I've just been guessing all morning about which way to walk."

"Good guessing." The voice sounded like it was winking. *"The gate to the path is just ahead."*

"You mean I was headed for it all along?"

"Don't be so shocked that you went right to it. You are a part of God, Michael Thomas of Pure Intent. Your 'guessing' is really what is called intuition, and your intuition will serve you well with a little more practice. I am here today only to help steer you," the voice paused. *"Look ahead, you are already at the gate!"*

Mike stood in front of a long row of bushes that ran between two rows of houses.

"I don't see anything."

"Look again, Michael Thomas."

Mike stared at the bush in front of him and slowly saw the outline of a gate through the leaves. It certainly blended in well! He looked toward the sky, and then back at the bush. There was the gate. Mike saw it even more clearly than he had just seconds before. Right before his own eyes it was changing. Now he couldn't help *but* see it, it was so obvious.

"What's happening?" Mike asked, dropping the bag from his shoulder.

"When you begin to see things you could not see before," the gentle voice said, *"you cannot go back and 'unsee' them. You will now see all gates clearly, since you gave intent for this one—you chose to see it."*

Although Mike didn't really understand what the angel meant, he was all too ready to get his journey rolling.

"This is a miracle!" whispered Mike as he continued to watch the tall bush transform into a real gate, opening up before him.

"Not really. Your spiritual intent just changed you, *and because you now vibrate at the same rate these things do, you can see them—no miracle. It's just the way things work here.*

"God is always and everywhere. Your human way of thinking only allows you to see and feel certain things. As you learn and change, you will begin to see and feel more things, and you may use your new understanding to make free choices. But you cannot 'unlearn' and go backward."

Mike was beginning to understand, but he had another question before he started down the path through the gate in front of him.

"You said I was a human with free will—I can make my own choices. Why can't I go backward if I want to? What if I want to just forget about all this and go back to my old life? Isn't that free choice?"

"Remember when you learned how to read? Once you could read, you could read about whatever you wanted, including all about your favorite baseball players on the backs of your trading cards. You did not have to wait to be told about those things—you could just go and read them for yourself. How could you not want to know how to read anymore? You are about to enter junior high school, Michael Thomas. You know too many things now to go back to being a first-grader again."

Mike knew he could turn around right now and go back to his old life. It was his choice. But every time he looked at the gate, he would want to walk through it, and he knew it would drive him crazy if he never did. Somehow it all made sense, and it was his choice to move forward, not backward—so Mike picked up the gym bag and went through the gate to begin his journey. There was a plain dirt path—it didn't look like anything special. But Mike was excited and he moved right on, quickly leaving the gate behind.

✳   ✳   ✳

No sooner had Mike gone through the gate then a shadowy greenish creature slipped through behind him. Leaves wilted where IT walked, and if Mike hadn't already moved on, the horrible smell would have let him know that something was behind him. IT quickly got on the road behind Michael Thomas, staying just out of sight but keeping pace with him. For as much as Mike was filled with excitement and a sense of adventure, IT was filled with hatred and the desire to destroy Mike. Mike had no idea that IT was there.

A short distance down the path, the land began to look a lot different than Mike's little town. There were no telephone poles and no highways. Mike even noticed that he hadn't seen any airplanes in the sky since he went through the gate. He'd eagerly started down the road without really thinking about where the path might lead, and now he realized that each step took him deeper into another world.

Mike wondered if this place was between Earth and Heaven, a special place for learning about how to be spiritual—to make him ready for the honor of going Home. The little path had slowly become wider and now was almost as wide as a road. There were no footprints at all, and it was very easy to follow.

Mike turned around suddenly. What was that? A dark green flash caught his eye as it darted to the left behind a boulder. *Must be a wild animal,* Mike thought. The road behind looked just like the road ahead, twisting and turning over hill after hill. There were beautiful green trees, lots of grass, and little rocky hills all around. Flowers of all colors were everywhere. It looked just like a picture.

Mike stopped to rest. He didn't have a watch, but he figured that it was about two o'clock in the afternoon, judging by the sun—time for food. He sat down next to the road and ate the left-over part of his breakfast and a cupcake he had packed in his bag. He looked around and noticed how quiet it was.

No birds, Mike thought. He studied the dirt at his feet. *No bugs, either. This really is a strange place.* He felt the sudden breeze in his hair. *At least there's air!* He looked up at the sky and saw the pure blue of a grand day.

His food was gone, but he knew the angel was out there and would provide for him somehow. He remembered that the Israelites roamed around in the desert for 40 years. At church, the minister said that food fell from the sky for the wandering people, and Mike had always wondered if the story was really true. *All those families following Moses probably had a bunch of rowdy kids just like there are now,* he thought. He could just see them turning to their parents, complaining, "Are we there yet? We've seen the same rocks a hundred times now, like we're going in circles! What's with that guy, Moses, anyway?"

Mike laughed at the thought, and then wondered if *he* was going to see the same rocks soon himself. He felt just like the one of the Israelites now—no clue where he was going and no food left to eat. It cracked him up.

Maybe the laughter was honored, or it was simply time, but around the next bend in the widening dirt road Mike saw it—the first house—and it was bright blue! *Good grief,* he thought. *If Mom could see this, she'd scream!* He chuckled to himself, *I've never seen such a blue house before.* The road actually led right up to its door, so he knew that it was supposed to be his first stop.

As Mike got closer to the small house, he could see that it was glowing softly from inside somehow. As he turned the path to go up to the door, he saw a small sign that said "House of Maps." Maps? That was what he'd asked for earlier! Now he was getting somewhere.

The door to the house opened suddenly, and out walked an angel that was the same beautiful blue as the house! It was huge, like the angel in his earlier vision—much bigger than a human. Its presence filled the air with a feeling of greatness and beauty, and again, the smell of flowers. The large blue one turned to him.

"Greetings, Michael Thomas of Pure Intent! We have been waiting for you."

Unlike the angel of his vision at the hospital, he could see this angel's face clearly—and it was full of peace and kindness.

Mike appreciated not being alone anymore and was very respectful.

"Greetings to you, too, O Great Blue One." Mike swallowed hard right away. What if the angel didn't want to be called blue? What if he only looked blue to Mike, and he really wasn't blue after all? Maybe he doesn't even like blue! Mike sighed at all the *what ifs* that ran through his young mind.

"I'm blue to everyone, Michael Thomas of Pure Intent," grinned the angel, "and I accept your greeting with joy. Please come into the House of Maps and get ready to stay for the night."

This time Mike was glad the angel had read his thoughts— or what was it the first angel had said? Angels could *feel* people's thoughts? Anyway, Mike was glad that he hadn't offended the keeper of the first house.

Mike and the blue angel, one small human and one very large angel, turned and entered the house. Even as the door shut behind them, two huge, wild, angry, red eyes peeked out from the thick bushes just to the left of the house's door. The eyes watched closely. They didn't get tired. They wouldn't move or even blink again until they saw Michael Thomas leave the Blue House.

Mike went into the house and was amazed by what he saw. On the outside, the house had looked pretty small and ordinary, but on the inside *it was huge!* It seemed to go on forever. He remembered that the white angel had said that *not everything is as it seems.*

Mike followed the giant angel through the huge halls. The place looked like an important library, like the one at the college where there were jillions of books. But there weren't any books or shelves. Instead, there were hundreds and hundreds of little holes in the walls, each hole containing what looked like a scroll of paper. The walls seemed as tall as the sky, and around every corner they turned, there was another hall with walls full of the same holes. He figured that the scrolls must be maps—after all, he was in the house of maps. But why were there so many scrolls? The walk around the giant rooms seemed endless, but Mike noticed that they seemed to be the only ones there.

"Are we alone?" Mike asked.

The angel turned and chuckled. "Depends on what you mean by 'alone,' I suppose. You're looking at the contracts of every person living on the Earth." The angel kept walking forward, smiling.

Mike stopped and asked, "What do you mean, 'contracts'?"

The large blue one stopped then, too, and said, "Michael, humans have many lessons to learn on Earth. To do so, they must live many times. Each time they are about to start a new life, they sit down and make a plan for that life. We call the plans *contracts*. The contracts outline what the humans want to learn, what they want to do to help others to learn, and when."

Mike stared, amazed that he was looking at the plans that every one of the people on Earth had made. The angel continued down the hall while Mike looked around. He stopped and turned, waiting patiently for Mike to look at everything.

There were ladders leaning up against racks that seemed as tall as skyscrapers. So many holes and so many contracts . . . holes all over the place.

"I still don't understand what this is all about, sir!" he exclaimed as he caught up to the angel.

"Before your journey is over, you will," the angel said softly. "There is nothing scary here, Michael. All is in order, as it should be. Your visit was expected, and I am honored to guide you. Your intent is pure, and we can see all that. Relax, and enjoy being loved by us."

The blue one's words helped Mike to feel a little calmer about being in such a strange place and hearing such strange ideas. There was so much love in those words, and he could feel every bit of it. "It's a grand feeling to be loved, isn't it, Michael?" The blue angel had returned to Mike's side and was towering over him.

"What is this feeling?" Mike asked softly. "I almost feel like I'm going to cry."

"You're changing again, Michael—what we call shifting into another vibration."

"I don't understand what that means. Uh . . . do you have a name, sir?" Mike hoped again that he wasn't upsetting the blue angel—he had called the angel "sir," but what if it was a woman angel? Should he have said "ma'am"?

"Just call me Blue," said the angel, winking. "I'm not a he or a she, but my size and voice tell your mind that I'm a he. Call me a *he*. It's okay." The angel paused to let Mike take it all in.

"Now . . . about that vibration shift," the blue angel continued. "The cells of your body are built, Michael, so that you can live in many vibratory rates. It's like being a radio. You can turn the knob to many different stations, or vibratory rates, that are called frequencies. All with the same radio. The vibratory rate you're used to is, let's say, station one. On this trip, however, you'll need to move up to station six or seven. Right now you're passing into what I'll call rate two. Each vibratory rate helps you act more God-like, as you've been told. And what you're feeling is love. Love is thick, Michael, so thick you can feel it, and it is powerful. Your new vibratory rate is letting you feel love more than you ever have before. Love is what Home is all about, and you'll feel it stronger and stronger with each house you visit."

Mike listened carefully to Blue. "Are you a teacher?"

"Yes, I am, Michael. Each House Angel you will meet on your journey is a teacher. When we're finished, you'll have a much better understanding of how things work in the Universe. Through your good intent, you have earned the privilege to learn all these things. You will receive your contract map here in my house. I'll give it to you early tomorrow, before you continue on the road. My house is first because it will help you with the rest of your journey. For now, please enjoy the gifts of food and rest."

Mike again followed Blue, who was starting to feel like a good friend—but a very blue one. They went into a wonderful indoor garden, where there were rows upon rows of fruits and vegetables. There were round windows in the roof, just as there had been in the other rooms. With all the bright light streaming in, it felt like outdoors. He could also smell bread baking somewhere in the house.

Everything was well taken care of, but still there was no one but Blue in sight. Mike was very curious.

"This house is enormous, but so far, you're the only one I've seen here. Who takes care of it all? Is all of this food just for one angel?" he said, pointing to rows of fruit growing plump in the garden.

"This garden is here only for the humans who are on the same journey you are, spending time here learning, passing through. I don't eat. Many take care of the garden—you just don't see them now. You'll always have food, shelter, and good health while you walk your path of learning. It's our way of honoring you and your good intent."

It's great to be so well cared for, Mike thought as he and Blue walked down a hall toward other rooms. Soon they came to a bedroom—a private little space with a high extra-soft bed and beautiful bright white sheets. Even the pillows were big and fluffy. Mike was so tired that he just wanted to jump into it and fall asleep immediately. He was impressed by all the work someone must have done to get all of this ready.

"All of this is for me?"

"You and others, Michael. It is prepared for all of those who have your same good intent," the angel smiled.

In the next room was a feast! Mike had never seen more delicious-looking food in one spot—much more than a kid could eat.

"Eat what you wish, Michael. What you can't eat won't be wasted. But don't tuck any away for the road. You'll want to, but don't do it. I've already told you that you'll always have food for your journey, and this is a test of your faith that you'll always be helped. You'll understand this better later."

Blue left the room. Mike dropped his bag and made a pig of himself on the wonderful food. He was very hungry from his day of travel. Soon his eyelids started to droop.

Oh, if I could feel like this forever! Mike thought. *I wouldn't mind being a human.* Mike got up, thinking that he'd clean up the table and the dishes in the morning. He was so tired! He quickly changed out of his clothes and hung them up on the little blue wall hooks. There was a fresh pair of pajamas laid out on the bed for Mike. He put them on and fell into the soft bed. He was asleep almost immediately.

✳ ✳ ✳

In the morning quiet, Mike woke up feeling amazingly rested. He washed up and went into the dining room, only to find that all the mess from the night before was already gone and a wonderful breakfast was there in its place! That's why he'd smelled eggs, potatoes, and delicious bread while he was waking up!

Mike enjoyed his breakfast alone. As he ate, he asked himself again if he was doing the right thing, leaving his family behind just because he was tired of being human. *Is it wrong to want to be out of my Earth life? What about the people I leave behind? They're stuck in the old life, while I get to experience this wonderful new place. It doesn't seem fair.* Now he started to feel sad for his family and schoolmates and Bryan.

What's happening? he wondered. *This actually hurts! I'm starting to feel sorry for what others don't have. Does this mean I've made the wrong decision? Should I go back to my old life?*

"It was bound to happen, Michael, that you should ask yourself that question." Blue suddenly appeared in the doorway and knew at once what Mike was feeling. Blue surprised Mike, but Mike was happy to see him and greeted him with a nod.

"I need some help here. I'm beginning to wonder if I've done the right thing," Mike said, looking down at his shoes.

"The way Spirit works is wonderful, Michael Thomas of Pure Intent. You are on a journey of learning. The important thing to remember is that you have to take care of yourself first. You can't give from an empty cup. There are many things for you to learn now. Later you will be better able to help everyone else."

"This is confusing, Blue. I'm not used to thinking about any of this."

"Even though you don't understand at this moment, Michael, your being here affects others—giving them chances to make their own choices—chances they would not have had if *you* had not chosen to be right here, right now. Trust that these things are true, and don't be so hard on yourself."

Mike was relieved that Blue took some of the pressure off. He knew Blue was telling him the truth, and he had more time to try to understand all of this. He picked up his gym bag and exited the wonderful dining room, stepping into the great hallway that led to the front door. The hugeness of everything still amazed him.

Blue walked slowly behind Mike. The zipper of Mike's bag was slightly open, but Blue didn't say a word about the muffin and bread sticks he saw peeking out.

"Where are we going? Should I keep going this way?" Mike asked, looking back. He knew he was about to receive his very own map, and he wanted Blue to lead the way.

"You may stop now." The two paused in the middle of a grand blue hall, and Blue silently walked over to a far wall near a ladder. "Come over here, Michael."

Mike did, and before long he was climbing a very tall ladder to find the exact hole where his map scroll was kept. He noticed as he climbed that above each hole was a name, and next to each name there was some strange writing. Mike knew that the holes were arranged in a certain way, but couldn't tell how because he didn't know what the unusual letters spelled. But Blue knew the arrangement and had told him exactly where to look for his hole, and Mike was now just a few feet from it.

Finally, he spotted it. The hole was marked "Michael Thomas," along with the foreign symbols—*probably angel language,* Michael thought to himself. Blue had told him that he was to get his map and get back down the ladder, and that he was not to touch anything but his own map. Mike had just started down the ladder when he spotted another group of names and his heart stopped. There were maps for his mom and dad here, too! The maps were arranged by family groups! *So that's the deal.* Mike knew he was absolutely forbidden to touch another's map, but he stopped to read some of the other names in his family group. They didn't make any sense to him. *Who are these other people?* he wondered.

"Michael?" Blue's voice floated up from below.

"Coming, Blue." Mike was embarrassed. He knew that Blue knew his thoughts, the questions he'd like to ask. He made his way quickly down the long blue ladder. As he handed the map over, Blue gave him a long look. Mike could see in Blue's eyes that there were no secrets, and that Blue was not mad. Mike felt another wave of love come from Blue. Mike was starting to feel that words were no longer needed! It seemed that he could say everything he wanted to Blue without saying it out loud. *This is weird!*

"Not as strange as what you're about to see," replied Blue to Mike's thoughts.

Blue put the small map scroll on the table. He then turned and faced Mike. "Michael Thomas of Pure Intent," Blue formally stated, "this is your life map. It will be with you from now on, one way or another. It is given in love and will be one of the most valuable items you will own."

Mike had to ask, "Is the map current?"

"More than you might want it to be," said the grinning blue one.

Blue handed the map to Mike and wordlessly invited him to examine it for himself. Mike took it and held it to his chest for a minute with pleasure and excitement. He felt the sacredness of the moment and opened the map like it was a ceremony. Blue smiled, because he knew what was coming.

All of Mike's pleasure and excitement left him when he opened the scroll. It was blank! Well, almost blank. Right in the middle of the map was a group of letters and symbols that he could just barely see. Mike bent over and stared at them. An arrow pointed to a small dot. Next to the dot were some words *You Are Here* and a small symbol for the House of Maps. Drawn around the dot were some trees and grass, and the dirt road Mike had traveled, but then it stopped! The map only showed Mike where he was right at that moment, with an area that looked about the size of a football field around it.

Mike was crushed. "Is this some kind of angel joke, Blue? I've come all the way to the House of Maps to receive a wonderful sacred scroll that only tells me that *I'm in the House of Maps?*"

"Things are not always as they seem, Michael Thomas of Pure Intent. Take this gift and keep it with you." Blue didn't really answer his question at all.

Mike knew it wouldn't do any good to ask the question again, so he rolled up the useless map and put it in the special pouch Blue held out to him. He was very disappointed. Blue led the way back to the front door and they stepped outside into the fresh air.

The angel faced Mike. "Michael Thomas of Pure Intent, there is one question that I must ask before you continue on your journey Home."

"What is it, Blue?"

"Michael Thomas of Pure Intent, do you love God?" Blue was very serious.

Mike thought it strange that the other angel had asked him the same question—in almost the same way. He wondered what that meant.

"Dear Blue Teacher, since you can see my heart, you know that I do love God." Mike stood and faced the angel as he gave his honest answer.

"So it is," said Blue, and with a smile and a wink, he stepped back into the small blue house and closed the door firmly. Mike thought it was really weird that the angel didn't have anything else to say. *Do these guys ever say good-bye?* he wondered.

$$* \quad * \quad *$$

The weather was sunny and pleasant. Mike picked up his bag and the map pouch and started down the dirt road. He laughed out loud as he remembered his visit to the House of Maps. *What kind of map only tells you where you are at this very minute? How useless. Of course I know where I am! What a crazy place this is.*

Laughter echoed back from the hills as Michael Thomas of Pure Intent laughed and talked out loud to the trees and rocks along the way. His laughter also fell on the wart-covered green ears of a very dark creature hanging back just behind him on the road. Mike had no idea that this dark shape had waited patiently for him to continue his journey and was again following his every step. IT didn't belong here. IT didn't need to eat or sleep. IT had no joy. IT made up its mind that Michael Thomas would never, ever reach the last house, and IT was getting closer and closer.

*   *   *   *   *   *

Chapter Five

The Second House

A little farther up the road, Mike could clearly see a problem. In the distance, he could see a fork in the road—he'd have to *choose* the way to the next house. To make matters worse, he had the feeling he was being watched. He stopped and scratched his head, staring down each of the two paths.

What is this? he thought to himself. *How am I supposed to know my way around here? I'm just a kid stuck with a bogus map.* Mike didn't expect any answers, since he was really just talking to himself, but he was upset.

He decided to check the map anyway, and sat down beside the road. He took the map pouch that Blue had given him off his shoulder and was about to pull out the map when he was almost knocked down by a horrible smell. *What* is *that!*

It smelled so bad he almost didn't want to see what it was. Something was definitely rotten, and he could only guess that it must be the bread he'd stashed away. He was right.

Mike gently removed the map from its pouch. Even though the map seemed useless, he knew it was sacred and didn't want it to get messed up. It was okay! Next, Mike pushed the gym bag several inches away and slowly unzipped it, half afraid of what he might find. He turned it over and carefully dumped everything out of it. He couldn't believe what he saw.

There on the ground were crumbs and clumps of a muffin and bread sticks that looked like they'd spent a long time outside rotting. They were black with mold. Then Mike saw the first and only bugs of this strange land—thousands of them! He stood up quickly, thinking, *How can this be? I just left the Blue House a few hours ago! Even rotting meat wouldn't do this. What's happening?*

Holding his nose, Mike stooped and took a closer look. The black wiggling lumps continued rotting right before his eyes. He watched as the tiny bugs ate the rest of the black mess—and then each other! Mike was grossed out and turned his head away. That was when he saw something behind him move.

Yes, there is something there! Mike knew he'd seen something green and blurry hide from him in the bushes! Chills went up and down his spine. His intuition warned him that it was dangerous to go back and see what it was, so he stayed there on the road.

Mike turned back to check out the smelly lumps and saw only dust! No bugs, no bread, no smell. It had all completely turned to dust, which was beginning to blow away in the gentle wind.

What does this mean? Mike wondered. Blue had warned him not to take any food, but he didn't think a little snack would be a problem! Maybe everything in the angel houses was somehow different and couldn't last very long out here on the road.

Mike looked through his bag to make sure that the disgusting mess hadn't ruined any of his things. But everything seemed untouched. He picked up the bag and smelled it. There was nothing left of the horrible smell! He had no idea what had really happened but had learned a valuable lesson: He would never again take food from any house on the road!

Something moved behind him again! Alarms were starting to go off in Mike's head. *Get moving!* He didn't know which way to turn. He automatically picked up the map, hoping it would give him a hint about which way to turn at the fork in the road—left or right? Again, the red *"You Are Here"* dot appeared on the map, showing nothing but the spot where he was standing at that moment. The two different paths didn't even show up on the sorry thing!

"Some map, Blue!" Mike exploded out loud. The sharp sound felt all wrong in this land, but Mike was upset and afraid. He stuffed the map back into its pouch.

Again, he saw movement out of the corner of his eye. *Is it getting closer? What is it?* Mike began to panic. He quickly got up and walked forward, looking over his shoulder after every other step.

The quick shape didn't show itself when Mike looked back. How could it know exactly when Mike was going to look? Mike walked a little bit faster until he was actually speed walking. The thing behind him walked faster, too! Mike made the short distance to the road's fork faster than he'd traveled anywhere so far in this puzzling land. He was sweating.

There Mike was, still not knowing which way to go, and upset that he couldn't decide. He stood there—heaving with panic—so scared and helpless that he shouted at the clouds.

"Blue! Which way?"

Mike didn't really expect to hear from Blue, so the familiar voice that seemed to come from inside his head was a shock.

"Use the map, Michael. Quickly!"

The urgent tone of Blue's voice convinced Mike not to question the command, even though the map was no help just a few minutes earlier. Again, he quickly rolled out the map. The red *"You Are Here"* dot seemed to be in the same place. It never moved, always staying in the center of the map. But something was different . . . Mike looked closer, and drops of his sweat fell onto the paper.

The fork in the road had appeared on the map! Mike remembered Blue saying that the map was always current—and now, since he was actually standing at the fork, the map changed to show his new position! Mike looked even closer at the map. Now there was also an arrow clearly pointing to the right!

Mike didn't hesitate. While rolling up the map, he scampered in the direction the arrow had pointed and made his way up a small hill. He looked back often, and he could feel the presence of a stalking shadow just out of sight. The green blur dashed between rock and bush, keeping up with Mike.

Just over the hill, Mike sighed in relief as he saw the next house in the distance. He'd be safe soon. He walked even faster now—still checking behind him—to the house where he knew he would find safety, a comfortable bed—and food.

The dark and evil creature behind Mike was furious! If Mike had stayed on the road just a moment longer, IT would have caught him! IT heaved with rage at the missed opportunity. IT found a place high in the trees outside the bright orange house that Michael Thomas had just entered. There, the foul creature patiently waited. It would be a long wait, but IT didn't care.

✳   ✳   ✳

Just inside the door of the Orange House stood another angel. Mike almost fell backwards when he saw the great being. The angel was as orange as the house!

"Greetings, Michael Thomas of Pure Intent! We have been expecting you," said the angel.

"Greetings back to you!" Mike hoped he didn't sound as out of breath as he actually was. His voice was a little shaky. He was so relieved that he had to stop himself from hugging the huge orange angel that now stood in front of him. Mike was glad to be protected and safe again.

"Come this way," said the orange angel, as he turned and led Mike into the House of Gifts and Tools. Mike made sure the door was closed tight. He followed the angel. He was still shaking a bit from his ordeal on the road, but now he was filled with more questions than ever about this puzzling land.

Like Blue and the glowing white angel before him, this orange angel was magnificent. The angel made him feel as welcomed and loved as the other two angels he'd met so far.

I guess they're all made of the same stuff, Mike said to himself.

"Actually, we're all in the same family. You may call me Orange," replied the great angel.

Mike couldn't believe he'd so quickly forgotten that there were no secrets with these angels—they all knew his thoughts.

"I'm sorry," was all Mike could get out of his mouth.

Orange turned and stopped. He tilted his head to one side questioningly. "Sorry? For complimenting me on my magnificence? For feeling loved? For wondering who we are?" The angel smiled. "There have been many visitors to this second house, Michael Thomas, and so far you've asked the fewest questions."

Mike sighed, "The day is just beginning." He wanted to ask the angel about the fear and panic he'd just run from out on the road. What was following him?

Of course, the angel knew the question was coming. "I cannot tell you what you wish to know, Michael."

"Can't, or won't?" Mike asked respectfully. "I know that you must know. Why won't you tell me about it?"

"You know more about IT than I do," the angel replied.

"How do you figure?"

"Things are not what they seem here."

"Will IT be there when I leave this house, Orange?"

"Yes, it will."

Mike put his head down. He thought for a moment about the angel's answer. "Does it live here? It seems out of place in this spiritual land."

"IT has the same right to be here as you do, Michael."

"Can it hurt me?" Mike asked, with a hint of fear in his voice.

"Yes."

"Well, Orange, what can I do to protect myself? Will you please help me?"

"That's why I'm here." The angel stood quietly smiling, and Mike suddenly stopped asking questions.

Mike began to relax. *I know that I'm safe now. This angel seems to want to help me, and there's surely more for me to learn. I'll take it easy and be patient. I'll be shown more as I go along. That seems to be how things work here.* Not more than an hour ago, Mike had thought the map was useless, and now it had saved him just in time.

"God is very current, you know," said the angel, almost laughing. He was once again tuning in to the thoughts of Michael Thomas. Orange turned and began to lead Michael farther into the house.

"I'm getting used to how things work here," Mike said as he walked. "It's what you need only when you need it. Right?"

"Something like that. In your old life of the lower vibration, Michael, time just passes in a straight line. It's like traveling on a ruler. Time for angels doesn't pass in the same way."

"So how *does* time pass for you?" As they spoke, Mike was being led through what seemed to be a warehouse. Like the Blue House, the inside of the Orange House was absolutely huge. Mike's jaw dropped as he saw rows and rows of wooden boxes stacked up to a ceiling that had to be 50 feet high.

"We don't have a yesterday or a tomorrow. There is only now. Time for us is like standing in the center of a big game board, which is lying flat on the ground. We can always see the whole board, since it's always under us. We're always in the 'now' of our time. We always move around the center. Because your time is straight, and you are always moving only straight ahead, you never get to be just in the 'now'—you look behind you to see where you have been, then you look ahead to see where you are going. You never get to just *be*. Instead, you always *do*. It's the way of your old world, but that's what works best for that world."

"That would explain the map then." Mike remembered that the red *"You Are Here"* dot was always in the middle, and that everything that happened to him always happened around that one spot. *It's exactly the opposite of a human map,* Mike thought.

"Correct!" said Orange over his shoulder as he walked ahead. "In your time, the map already has all the roads and towns on it, and they don't move—the human does all the moving. But when you get closer to *our* vibration and time, *you* are the red dot on the map and the roads and houses right around you only appear on the map as you reach them—*they* do all the moving, not you. So, as you stop on your journey, you're the red dot, and everything that is right around you will appear on the map, and then you will know what to do."

Mike had to really think about this one. It was confusing, but at the same time, it made sense. What happened to Mike back at the fork in the road proved to him how important the map really was, even if it didn't work like the ones he was used to. He knew that the next time he had to make a choice like that, he wouldn't worry about it until he had to—then the map would work. He was beginning to understand what his mom meant when she said, "We'll cross that bridge when we come to it."

Just as Blue had done in the Blue House, Orange led Mike in and out of many beautiful rooms and hallways on their way to what would be Mike's room during his stay. No holes lined the hallways of this house, though. Instead, there were more rows of wooden boxes with names on them in that same strange writing . . . Mike knew that somewhere there was a box with his name on it and he'd see it soon.

"This is your room, Michael. Tomorrow we'll begin. Your meal is ready and waiting and will be served in the room to the right." With that, Orange closed the door to Mike's room and left.

Mike stared at the closed door. *You might be an angel, but you don't seem to have very good manners,* he thought to himself after Orange left without saying good-bye. *I guess I can't expect them to act like humans.* Mike set down his bag and went into the next room for dinner.

Mike ate until he was full. The food was as wonderful here as it was at the House of Maps. He noticed that the fork and knife were carved out of wood and had beautiful designs on them. When he was done, he felt strange leaving the mess of plates and bowls out, but he knew that as it had been in the Blue House, there were others here who'd straighten up after him. *A place full of wonderful angels, yet here they are, taking care of humans.*

Mike started to wonder where the toilet was in this house, then it hit him: He hadn't been to the bathroom for days! He didn't even remember having the urge to go after passing through the gate! His body was apparently changing in this surprising land. *How weird,* he thought. Sure enough, there was no toilet in the little room!

✳   ✳   ✳

In the morning, Mike woke up feeling great. He hopped into his clothes and ran to breakfast. Again, he dined alone. The fresh fruit and warm breads were more delicious than any he'd ever tasted. He picked up an apple and examined it closely, but it looked just like the red apples his mom used to pack in his lunch. *So why does it taste so much better?* Mike wondered. *I'll have to ask Orange about this.*

"The food is in *our* time," said a cheerful Orange from the open door of the room. The angel had just arrived and had heard Mike's thoughts.

"It cannot exist in a slower vibration," Orange went on. "You have already noticed that your body is different here. You are a human traveling in a land of angels, yet you can exist here because your vibration has changed to a faster rate. It is the same with the food. Angels don't eat food; it is only here for you. It is made just moments before you are ready to sit down and eat, and vibrates at a certain rate during that time so that you will have something to eat while you are here with us. It lasts only long enough for you to eat it. That is why there is no need to go to the bathroom, and why you can't stash it away in your bag for a snack later. There is no trash here, Michael—with the food or your body."

"Well, that explains *that,*" Mike blushed. The disgusting mess on the road earlier almost got him into trouble.

The angel led Mike out of the dining room and into what looked like a rodeo arena. The light was very bright there. Several wooden boxes had been opened, and there were a few orange benches for humans to rest on. There were strangely shaped packages, too.

"Welcome to the House of Gifts and Tools, Michael Thomas of Pure Intent. Please take a seat. You'll be here for a while. This is the first of many classes. After each teaching session will come a practice session, then a test. You will spend three weeks in this house learning to use the gifts and tools of this new spiritual vibration."

"You are learning much and raising your vibration, Michael Thomas," Orange said again and again during the classes. "These are the gifts and tools we promised to give you to help you on your journey. They are yours only because of your pure intent. You cannot go on to the next houses without knowing how they all work, though, and you absolutely cannot go Home unless you use them very well."

Mike had been told that this training would come and that it would prepare him to go Home. He paid close attention as Orange presented him with several gifts. They didn't look like any gifts he'd ever seen before, though. There was no little box, no wrapping paper. Mike watched as balls of intense orange light appeared in Orange's right hand. The balls of light took shape—they looked like magnificent crystals! A sound came from each one . . . the sound of energy singing! Mike could *feel* the sound.

As each crystal gift was presented to Mike, Orange held it to Mike's heart and put his left hand over his own chest. The gift would then disappear into Mike's body, leaving Orange's hand empty. This was such a wonderful ceremony and it all felt so sacred.

When the gift giving was done, Orange said lovingly, "Michael Thomas of Pure Intent, I present you with these gifts because you have earned them. You have crossed over what we call 'The Bridge of Swords.' You walked through the gate in the bush and stayed on your journey with the intention of becoming your true spiritual self—going Home. These are gifts of the

Third Language, the language of Spirit. You will be able to hear the angels speak to you more easily as you travel to each of the remaining houses. You will feel more connected to us and you will be able to feel the energy of Spirit stronger than ever, which is the beginning of the connection to Home. This happens slowly and naturally for all those who choose to cross the Bridge of Swords."

So he could be sure that Mike fully understood just how important these gifts were, Orange then had Mike explain to him what they were for. Spiritual matters were still new to Mike, so this wasn't easy, but he said what was in his heart and Orange was satisfied.

Then Orange explained how humans live many different times on Earth, going back again and again to learn certain lessons. He said that all humans brought special gifts with them to help them do what they were supposed to do during each life. Although Blue had mentioned this, it was still very new to Mike, and he was surprised to learn again that a person lived more than one life!

Orange went on to explain that it takes humans many lifetimes to learn all the lessons they need to learn and to get all of their "work" done. If something wasn't learned well enough earlier, then they have another chance. He called the lessons "karma," and explained that this helped humans learn, and also helped planet Earth. This was the way things worked for humans life after life. He told Mike that each time he learned one of the lessons that he'd brought in with him, he moved to a new vibration, then moved on to the next lesson until they were all learned. Those old lessons couldn't go with him on the way Home, just like the food here couldn't.

Mike suddenly saw himself as a rotting pile on the road—one that didn't pay attention to the teacher. He sat up straighter and listened even closer. He sure didn't want that to happen!

Orange saw Mike's thoughts and laughed out loud. And when Mike realized that once again Orange knew what he was thinking, he laughed, too. Mike was surprised by how close he felt to Orange. He was a wonderful teacher and a great buddy— even if he didn't know how to say good-bye.

Orange taught Mike how to think thoughts that would actually create energy. "This is how you control the world around you. Use your deep spiritual feeling and knowingness to place yourself where you'll be able to learn more lessons and help more people. That is called co-creation. You deserve this and you planned it."

Mike had no idea what that meant, but he did as he was told and apparently passed all the tests. The co-creation gift was absorbed into his body, along with another gift that helped him clear up some things from other times he'd lived. He and Orange had a little celebration to honor the gifts and talked about each of them, so they'd work better. They passed into him like ghosts through a wall and became like parts of his body!

Mike felt as if he were studying to be one of those little monks he saw on a TV show once about Tibet. Each time he would repeat what Orange had taught him, he could feel Orange actually looking at his heart! Orange could be intense, and during these times when Mike made promises and agreed to accept each of the gifts placed into his spiritual power center, Orange seemed to be reading his soul. He was uneasy at first, but then he understood that Orange was just making sure that his words matched his heart. If he'd been faking it, Orange would have known immediately and would have stopped Mike in his tracks.

Day after day, packages were opened, explained, and joined into Mike's spiritual self. There were a few tests, too. One was especially hard. Mike had been afraid of small spaces for as long as he could remember. One time at the grocery store, when he was very little, everyone was pushing and shoving in the check-out line. Mike was jammed between his mom and another lady and felt as if he couldn't breathe. He cried so loud that he scared everybody, including himself! One of the gifts from Orange was the power to beat this fear.

Mike agreed to receive the gift. Orange told him that the feeling of panic in close spaces was a "karmic overlay," and getting rid of the fear would clear up any of the problems he may have brought into this life from other lives.

A few days later, Orange opened a large crate. Instead of taking something out, a very loving Orange asked Mike to step in! The lid was closed, and the dark was thick around Mike as he crouched in the box. The pounding of each nail was loud and scary as Orange hammered the lid tight. Then it was very quiet and very dark.

He could clearly hear himself breathe in the small space, and he was so cramped he could scream. He could even hear his heart beating. Orange didn't explain. He didn't have to; it was another test that Mike couldn't fake.

For about ten seconds, Mike's heart raced. Then, when his entire body should have been shaking with the fear, the feeling completely went away and he relaxed! The gift had worked! The fear tried to take over, but Mike's new spirit had stopped it. He felt very peaceful and sang some songs to himself and finally fell asleep. An hour later, Orange opened the box and let Mike tumble out.

"You're amazing, Michael Thomas of Pure Intent!" said the huge angel with a huge smile. Mike could actually feel how proud Orange was of him. "Not all make it this far." This was the first time Mike actually realized that he wasn't the only one who'd asked to go Home. The subject had come up before, but he just didn't get it until now.

During the last week of training, Orange brought out a very large crate. "There are three tools you will need for your journey," Orange said with great ceremony. He went over to the special crate and opened it. Each time Orange opened a package or crate, Mike would sit up straight on his bench, wondering what was coming next—everything was so amazing! Even so, he wasn't ready for what Orange had now to give him.

Orange's back was toward Mike, so he couldn't see what the angel had taken from the crate. As the angel turned to present the first tool, Mike caught a flash of something silver—Orange was holding a huge sword!

"Behold the Sword of Truth," stated the orange angel as he presented the weapon to Michael Thomas.

If it looked big when the angel held it, it looked *giant* when Mike did. It was heavy beyond belief and really hard to balance. He couldn't believe this was happening. "This is a real sword!"

"As real as the other gifts, Michael. This is only one of three that you'll carry with you on the outside of your body as you travel to the next four houses."

Michael held the sword for some time. He studied its beautiful designs, which looked to have a spiritual meaning. He guessed that his name was somewhere in all the beautiful, strange writing. The handle was large and long, with the grip itself worked of a bright blue stone. The blade gleamed mightily and was very sharp on both of its edges. The sword was so magnificent that it took his breath away! And now it was his!

"Try to swing it." Orange stepped back.

The sword felt alive in his hands and almost swung itself! Mike fell down with the power of it, and felt stupid and clumsy as he got up to try again.

Orange held up his hand to stop Mike. "Here, see if this helps." The angel went to the crate again and brought out something else. Again, the new object flashed silver lightning as it came out of the crate. A huge shield!

Mike shook his head in disbelief. *Wow! Spiritual gifts? Weapons of war? Am I being trained to be a knight in shining armor, like one of King Arthur's knights?*

"Everything is not as it seems, Michael Thomas of Pure Intent." Orange stood before him with the shield in his hands, answering his confused thoughts. "Try this."

Orange showed him how to strap the shield to his arm, then gave him a few tips on how the shield and the sword balanced each other's weight so that it was possible to swing the sword without falling over—a good thing to learn.

"Michael, this is the Shield of Knowledge of Spirit. Together with the Sword of Truth, the balance is all-powerful! Darkness can't live where there is knowledge. No secrets can live in the light, and there is light when you acquire knowledge and learn the truth of it. There's no greater combination than this. Knowledge and Truth *must* be used together."

"Anything else in that crate?" Mike joked as he almost fell over again with the heavy sword and shield.

"Funny you should ask!" Orange went back to the crate. Mike's jaw had dropped right open. The angel reached down and picked up an object that was even larger than the rest, with silver lightning flashing again as he held it up for Mike to see.

"Behold the Armor of Wisdom!" exclaimed a very amused orange angel, almost laughing at the expression on Mike's face.

"I don't understand!" Mike sat down sadly on the bench. "I'm just a kid. How in the world can I be expected to carry all this?"

"With practice. Here, let me show you." Orange took the sword and shield. He helped Mike put on the heavy Armor of Wisdom, its beautiful designs like those on the sword. It was like a vest and covered Mike down to his waist. As he put each arm into it, it went on like a glove—a perfect fit! Orange put a belt around Mike's waist that was specially made to hold the Sword of Truth. Then he showed Mike how to carry the heavy Shield of Knowledge with a special hook on his back for traveling.

When all was complete, the angel again stood back.

"Michael Thomas of Pure Intent, you now have the three tools that will let you pass into the new vibration. You have the Sword of Truth, the Shield of Knowledge, and finally—the Armor of Wisdom. The armor is also called the 'Mantle of God.' It represents the wisdom you'll need to use the other two tools correctly. Tomorrow you'll start your training as a Warrior of the Light. There is great power in the three. You must *always use them together!*"

Orange took the weapons from Mike and led him back to his room so he could wash, eat, and go to sleep. Mike lay in bed for a very long time wondering about all the things he'd seen in this great land so far. He dozed off with thoughts whirling in his mind.

In the morning, Mike again found himself in the Hall of Training. It was during the next few days that Orange began to show Mike how to use the old weapons with some skill. The first practice was balance. He made Mike run up and down stairs in full battle dress—sword out and shield ready. He showed Mike how to fall and get up quickly by using the shield as a counterweight to balance himself. Through all of this, Mike noticed that the tools never got dirty, and they never became dented or scratched.

Mike ran with the tools, walked with them, twirled with them, did everything but fight with them. He was slowly getting the feeling of balance.

After a few days, an odd thing happened. At night when he took off the battle gear, Mike didn't feel more comfortable. Instead, he felt small and helpless and much too light!

At least a week went by before Orange began the final training on how to actually use the Sword of Truth. Mike expected Orange to turn into some kind of karate master and teach Mike how to fight. Instead, Mike got a completely different kind of training.

"Now you're ready to learn how to use the weapons, Michael Thomas. Draw your sword."

With a flourish that would have made any knight proud, Mike easily swung the long sword. The angel watched with approval. "Now raise it to God."

Mike did as he was told.

"Before you speak your truth, Michael Thomas, feel the sword."

Mike didn't have any idea what Orange meant. *Feel the sword?* It was in his hands, and it was heavy. How could he *not* feel the sword?

"Michael Thomas of Pure Intent," said the intense Orange one, "hold the sword up high and speak your truth. Do you love God?"

There was that question again! Only this time, he was holding a huge spiritual weapon pointed toward heaven, and he was supposed to give some kind of speech? Just the same, he started to give his usual answer. "Yes, I do, Orange. As you can see, my heart—"

Mike couldn't finish. The sword was starting to vibrate! It was almost singing as it sent an intensely warm vibration up his arm and into his chest. The shield was humming in answer to it, and the armor was growing warm, too! They were all working together. The tools he'd gotten so used to carrying were somehow alive with his intent! Then he remembered that he was speaking.

"I do most certainly love God!" Mike held the sword up high, and it vibrated even stronger with his truthful intent! The power of these tools filled him and made him feel like he could stand there forever, weapons ready, intending his purpose to go Home where he belonged. The music of the three went straight to his heart and sent tears flowing down his face. The tools were accepting his body, joining with his Spirit because he had pure intent! So this was the reason for the sword, shield, and armor? Now he felt even wiser and more determined to finish his journey.

Orange and Michael Thomas spent the evening together like best friends. Mike knew it was almost time to leave. He never did learn how to actually fight, but thought it was because the weapons were only symbols. He asked Orange about Home and the road that led to it. During his training time, he'd wondered why he was being taught with Earth weapons of war in such a sacred land as this.

"There is much more that you will have to learn before you will be able to understand the answer to your questions, Michael Thomas," Orange had told him.

"You sound like you're dodging the question, Orange, just like my dad does sometimes!" Mike teased.

That got a chuckle out of Orange. "I'm not dodging, Michael. There is just no answer for you until later."

"I feel really close to you, Orange." Mike was choking up. He dreaded having to leave this great master angel to go out on the road alone again.

"Say no more, Michael Thomas of Pure Intent. I'll share an angel secret with you." Orange bent down so that he could look Mike right in the eyes, and continued. "You and I—we are of the same family. We don't say good-bye because we never leave one another. I'm always with you, and here for you. You'll see . . . now it's time for you to go to bed."

Mike appreciated Orange comforting him. But he had a hard time understanding how he could be in the same family as a great orange angel. Mike felt silly, realizing that Orange must have heard him that first night when he complained that angels never say good-bye. *What a thought! They never leave me!*

Mike remembered for the first time since he'd arrived at the Orange House three weeks ago that at the fork in the road, the angel Blue had somehow given him advice on how to use the map. He actually heard Blue's voice in his head.

"Orange, do you know Blue?"

"As I know myself, Michael."

Their session was over, so Mike went back to the room he was liking more and more, the place where he ate and slept. Even though there had been no talk of leaving, Mike found himself packing his things, getting ready to continue his journey in the morning. He looked for a while at his precious baseball cards and sighed with the memories. As much as they meant to him, they were beginning to feel out of place.

The next morning after his meal, Mike stood at the front door in deep, sad thought. Orange had led him there in silence. This time, though, Mike had quite a load to carry—along with his gym bag and his map, he now had the new tools swinging and clanking as he walked.

Orange could see that Mike would have a tough time managing all that—the battle gear was still too new to him.

"Michael, your journey would be so much easier if you left your bag behind."

"But all this stuff means a lot to me. I need it."

"For what?"

"For remembering all the great times I've had." Mike couldn't bear the thought of leaving his baseball cards and pictures behind.

"For connection to the old ways, Michael?"

These questions were very disturbing to Mike.

"Why don't you leave your bag with me, Michael? I love you, and I'll keep everything safe for you here."

"No!" Mike didn't want to hear any more about it. It was *his* stuff, and he'd hang on to it as long as he could. He needed something in this place to remind him of who he really was.

The angel had nothing else to say. He just shook his head.

Mike always got his way. He noticed that all the angels had let him make his own choices and never argued with his final decision.

Michael Thomas didn't say good-bye to Orange that morning. Standing on the steps facing the angel he'd been with for weeks, he remembered that you don't have to say good-bye to family here—in this land they're always with you.

"See you soon, Orange." Mike hoped he would, but didn't really believe it.

The great orange angel just went inside and shut the door.

✳   ✳   ✳

Mike was on the road again. It was all he could do to hold on to everything, his load was so heavy and hard to handle. The sword, shield, armor, and map pouch, along with his gym bag—it was almost too much. *What a dumb deal. I must look pretty ridiculous,* Mike thought. *Do I really need these weapons? I'll never use them in any battle. I don't know how, anyway . . . Orange never taught me. They're only for looks and ceremony, so I shouldn't have to drag them around, too.*

He was trying so hard to balance his teetering load that he'd forgotten all about the terrible trouble waiting for him on the road somewhere. A dark green danger was watching him from the trees, examining him with new interest. The old Mike was gone. Here was a new Mike who had weapons and power! This wasn't going to be easy anymore, and IT would have to make a new plan—one that would surely stop Michael Thomas. The dark one decided to continue to follow from a short distance behind, waiting for the chance to strike Michael Thomas of Pure Intent. IT was absolutely sure that this little human would never make it Home.

$$* \quad * \quad * \quad * \quad * \quad *$$

Chapter Six

The Great Storm

Mike had been on the road for less than two hours when he noticed that the wind was picking up and the sky was getting dark. *Oh, great! Storms in heaven.*

His load was giving him such a hard time that he'd already had to stop several times to rest. It was heavy, and he still couldn't balance it very well. This upset Mike deep down and made *him* feel out of balance—and now he'd have to deal with a storm, too! He had to find cover soon if it was going to rain. The last thing he needed was for his load to get wet and get even heavier . . . or for the battle equipment to rust.

He stopped again for a minute and looked behind him for the first time since he left the House of Gifts and Tools. IT was there! As fast as lightning, the green blur jumped to hide behind some big rocks. But this time Mike had seen it. IT was real . . . and huge! Dread swept over Mike's tired body as he realized that this thing hadn't gone away while he visited the last house. He couldn't forget that IT was dangerous and could hurt him, and he rested facing the road he'd just walked down so he could watch for it. He had to stay ready. He had no idea *how* ready.

The wind got stronger, and the going got much tougher. The new battle shield caught the wind almost like a sail, strapped to Mike's back as it was. Without his bag, he would have been able to keep the shield in the battle position Orange taught him—holding it against the wind he'd be able to balance himself and move much faster. But he couldn't. He'd have to find cover soon.

Mike had never seen anything like it. The weather was changing so fast! Always aware of the thing following him, Mike noticed that IT was getting closer even though the wind was so strong and the rain was coming down so hard. It was quick! *How can it move so fast?*

The weather was getting more and more terrible, forcing Mike to try to protect himself as much as he could until he could find a safe place farther up the road. Things were changing fast! He hunched down and struggled ahead, trying to resist the wind. Finally, he had to stop and huddle down on the ground—there was just no way he could walk now.

The storm seemed to be a horrible creature itself, the wind groaning and wailing. Where Mike's armor couldn't protect him, the rain felt like needles stabbing into his body, thrown straight at him by the strong wind. He was in big trouble.

Mike peeked back at the road behind him, which he could barely see through all the rain and fog. But he could clearly see the dark green figure, now standing tall, with eyes glowing a fiery red. IT was starting to move ahead! The storm didn't even slow it down! *How in the world . . . ?* Mike was afraid.

Then there was Blue's voice again, no mistake about it, as it called to Mike from inside his head. *"Use the map!"*

The voice is so clear! Mike thought. *Blue's surely with me.*

The storm's anger was way beyond any storm this small-town boy had ever seen. He felt as if he were trapped inside a tornado. He was crawling close to the ground now, trying his best not to be swept away by the unbelievable force of the storm. The flatter he could make himself, the better.

The storm's groaning and wailing had gotten so loud that Mike was afraid it might make him deaf! He was so scared that his fear almost stopped him right there on the road, but deep inside he felt that there was something different about this storm. He knew he had to look at his map. If only he could reach it! But it was all he could do just to stay alive.

The anger of the wind and the rain attacked every inch of him, and he was actually hanging on to plants with one hand and his precious gym bag in the other. The map pouch had been slung around his neck but was now smashed underneath him—it was safe, but there was no way to get to it. The violent, howling wind lifted his body up off the ground. The fierce storm was poking him and pushing him, trying to force him to lose his hold on the little plant. Using his last bit of strength, Mike drove the toes of his shoes into the mud and hung on to his tough little weed with his one free hand.

It was completely dark now; the huge piles of black clouds built by the storm covered Mike completely—and now he couldn't see at all. His eyes were just barely cracked open, as he was trying to keep out the attacking wind and rain. But there was nothing to see. Mike couldn't even see the ground beneath him! Where *was* the dark thing? Was IT coming to get him? Should he try to move, or would the storm blow him to his death?

Like bells in a fire drill, every cell in Mike's body sounded the alarm and vibrated with readiness as never before. Fear? No! His will to live and fight this out kept him going. He was determined. He had to find a way to get to the map!

"Michael Thomas, let go of the bag!" This time, it was Orange's voice that sounded powerfully inside Mike's head. Mike knew then that his choice was to either let go of the gym bag or die. His clothes were soaking wet now, even under the armor, and he was starting to shiver.

Through the screams of the attacking wind, Mike heard and felt a tremendous explosion. *What was that!* He even felt a vibration through the ground. IT had to be coming closer now, and Mike had to do as Orange had told him. IT was coming!

One by one, Mike uncurled the fingers that had been holding the bag so tightly. He was going to have to let the screaming winds take his valuable baseball cards, his precious pictures, and all the other treasures he had so carefully packed. But how could he let all of that go? There wouldn't be anything to remind him of the great times he'd had with Bryan, his family, and his classmates. It was his *life!*

He opened the last finger, and the bag was jerked away from him. His finger felt like it was broken. It hurt his heart to hear the bag tear open and the baseball cards and photographs flap as they were being blown away. It had taken him years to collect those cards!

The storm was as mean as an angry wrestler standing over him, smashing him into the ground. He thought for a minute that IT had finally caught up with him and had begun to beat him and tear him apart!

Soon the flapping sound was over, and he knew that all of his belongings were gone. Gone in an instant—and it made Michael Thomas angry. Everything that reminded him of the people he loved was scattered all over the place by a storm that only cared about beating him to death.

It didn't seem possible, but the storm got even louder. Without the bag to hold on to, Mike could use his hand now to reach his map. The strong wind lifted up his shield again, and he almost lost his grip. He grabbed at the map just as the wind lifted him up off the ground—and caught it! Inch by crawling inch, he managed to bring his arm and the map to his chest, dragging some dirt and grass along as well. He just had to see the red *"You Are Here"* dot.

Mike had scratched his hand on a rock trying to get the map unrolled, but how was he going to be able to SEE the map? It was pitch black—he couldn't see a thing! What if the writing was washed off? His arm was getting numb, and he could barely hang on. Mike was losing his grip.

* * *

The storm didn't hurt IT a bit. As a low-vibration visitor in a high-vibration land, the creepy creature didn't even feel the terrible wind and rain of the storm that pounded the ground all around it. IT stood up and easily made its filthy, dark way to the middle of the road, walking toward a flattened Michael Thomas who was being battered by the storm.

IT was not swayed in the least by the strong howling wind. The storm only made everything harder to see. As IT came closer, with the ease of someone taking a walk in the park, IT began to feel very lucky. But the darkness of the storm was a problem, and soon IT couldn't see any better than Michael Thomas could. No matter, though—IT was ready to finish him off. IT was ready to scatter his body all over this stupid fairyland that it hated so much.

Mike felt how close IT was now.

The darkness was like a blindfold but that didn't matter, because IT could sense where Mike was on the ground. IT attacked with great determination and power—only to find itself tearing apart a section of dirt very close to where Mike was lying.

Mike had heard IT, but IT had also heard something else— the tearing of the gym bag's fabric and the flapping of the base- ball cards. IT quickly turned to face the new sounds. Now IT knew where Michael was!

IT came closer and could barely make out the shape of a help- less Michael Thomas with one hand under him and one hand holding a small, sturdy weed. If IT could have smiled, IT would have at that moment.

IT jumped on Michael Thomas's back, slamming down with the force of a huge boulder. But instantly, a million darts stabbed the beast's wart-covered body. In a blinding flash of pure white light and a gleam of silver, IT was thrown back with tremendous power. IT flew back a long way through the air, as if it had been shot out of a cannon, and landed in almost the exact place where it had started!

The monster's skin was smoking from touching something extremely hot. IT tried to figure out what in the world had hap- pened. IT was very confused and weakened by the powerful force that had thrown it far from its target.

Mike's shield had been firmly strapped to his back, and it cov- ered most of his body. The very thing that Mike thought was going to weigh him down—his shield—had suddenly protected him! It had done its work even without Mike's knowing it. It was part of him. The dark creature's low vibration touching the high vibration of the shield had immediately caused a powerful reac- tion. The Shield of Knowledge had pushed off the terrible attack!

✳   ✳   ✳

Mike finally managed to bring the map up near his face. He looked down at it, hoping he might be able to see something despite the blackness. Suddenly, there was a flash of light! It felt like an especially violent blast of wind had hit him, but with it came a miracle—a light so bright that it lit up everything around him long enough for him to clearly see through his squinted eyes.

The section of map that Mike had so carefully unwrapped while the storm had raged was indeed visible! His eyes danced over it and quickly found the *"You Are Here"* dot. He ignored the smell of smoke and ozone around him. The map showed the road where Mike was crouched down, and pointed right around the corner to a cave. A few yards east, and he'd be safe!

Mike felt that God had brought him a close lightning strike in that needful moment. He never understood that it was IT, determined to destroy him, that caused the flash of light at just the moment he needed it. What had just happened was what Orange had called "co-creation"—being in the right place at the right time. But Mike could have never dreamed that the middle of a howling storm was the right place *that* day.

It took everything he had to crawl from weed to weed, rock to rock. It took almost 20 minutes—hugging the mud, flattened out by the fierceness of the storm—to reach the cave. All this work to travel only a few yards—but he had to do it. Even in almost total darkness, he found the entrance to the small cave that would be his protection against sure death. It was an incredible strain to pull himself bit by bit, but he thanked God with every inch that IT hadn't come any closer.

As he reached the cave, Mike heard the storm getting worse. He couldn't believe what he heard all around him. *There can be trouble even in this magical world!*

All was quiet in the cave, but Mike was a mess. His hand was bleeding where he'd scraped it on the rocks. Mud and dirt soaked his clothes, and it was very cold in the cave. Slowly, he got up and tried to figure out what had happened to him and what he should do next.

You might think at this point that Michael Thomas felt very thankful to escape the storm—and the mysterious enemy that had come so close to destroying him. Instead, he was angry! He shook, not from the cold, but from his sudden rage—all of his precious things had been ripped from him!

He knew that the angels controlled the weather here, and he yelled out in anger to any of them who would listen. "YOU TRICKED ME!" He went to the mouth of the cave and yelled at the howling wind. "DO YOU HEAR ME?" He felt as if the angels had turned on him.

"Now I see how it works!" he continued to shout. "When I didn't give up my bag as Orange suggested, you all just TOOK IT FROM ME ANYWAY!"

Mike couldn't stop shaking. He was so mad and so cold there at the mouth of the cave. Tears of hurt feelings ran down his cheeks. He cried hard until there were no tears left. He felt tricked and robbed.

A little fire started to flicker at the back of the cave, and Mike soon felt its warmth behind him. He turned to look as a gentle voice spoke.

"I gave you good advice, Michael Thomas of Pure Intent." Orange was standing by the little fire, inviting Mike to come back and warm himself.

Mike had calmed down, and slowly went over to the fire. He sat before it with his head down. After a few minutes, with tears still in his eyes, Mike began to ask some questions.

"Did all this have to happen?"

"No, Michael. That is the whole point."

"Why did you take away my things?"

"This is still a land of free choice, Michael Thomas. No matter what you think, the human is most important here, and the human is honored above all other creatures."

"Free choice! Orange, if I hadn't let go of my bag, I would have died!"

"Exactly right, Michael. You *chose* not to let the bag go when you had a chance earlier at my house. If you had done as I suggested, you would have learned more about these things. The bag would still be safe. Right now, you cannot understand the big plan of this place. But that's why *we* are here, and why the new gifts and tools were given to you."

"It wouldn't have hurt to keep a few of the things I loved. They meant a lot to me!"

"They didn't belong on your journey, Michael." Orange sat down on a rock beside the fire. "These things that you carried are the Earthly part of you. They drag you back to that old vibration and clash with the new vibration that you're studying and accepting. All of you is changing, Michael, and we know that you feel it."

"Why didn't you tell me this earlier? It would have saved me some trouble." Mike looked at his bleeding hand and ruined clothes.

"You chose not to let your bag go at the Orange House—so we had to teach you this way."

Mike began to trust the wisdom of what Orange said.

"If I hadn't let go, what would have happened?"

"You could not have gone ahead on the road carrying the old energy objects. The wind would have carried you back to a place of old energy. You would have been safe, but all that you had learned and received so far on this sacred path would have been lost. It would have been the death of the new Michael Thomas, and you would have left this place."

Orange paused for just a moment, then continued. "This is important, Michael Thomas of Pure Intent. You can't hold on to any part of the old energy—even what may seem precious—and still move ahead into the new energy. The old energy and the new energy cannot work together. Moving into the new energy means that you are moving into a new dimension. The rules of the old energy are different from the rules of the new."

Orange came closer to Mike. "Let me ask you this . . . do you still have love for Bryan, and good memories of him in your heart? Or did you lose all of that in the storm, too?"

"I still have it." Mike knew where this was going.

"Then what have you really lost, Michael?"

He realized what Orange was trying to teach him, and was silent.

As if he were a wise father answering a child's many questions, Orange continued. "The memories of your loved ones are in the energy of what you felt while you were with them. Memories are not held in any *things.* When you want to remember, then do so using all of the love and gifts we have given to the new Michael Thomas.

"When you start doing this, you'll even see that your feelings about your loved ones have changed. The gifts help you to have more wisdom and understanding about who your loved ones really are . . . and who *you* really are. Your memories are much better than the objects you collect to remind you of people. Remember, those things belong to the *old* Michael Thomas. The *new* Michael Thomas doesn't need them anymore."

All of this talk about Spirit was still new to Mike. It would be a while before he would understand all that Orange had told him.

"When you're finished with the seventh house," Orange smiled, "you'll have full understanding."

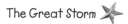

Mike understood that he couldn't carry those old energy things Home, but he was sad. He still felt a bit tricked by his angel friends because they hadn't just come right out and told him all of this earlier. He did remember the rotting food that had once been so delicious—and how Orange had explained that it was of an old energy and didn't belong on the road—but he hadn't realized that his prized possessions were of the same low vibrational energy!

Then Mike realized that he'd now been given *two* suggestions along the way: one by Blue not to take food for the road, and one by Orange to leave his bag behind. Both times he didn't take the angels' advice, and both times he had gotten himself into trouble.

Mike made up his mind to listen more closely to what the angels told him along the way. This was a strange place with rules he didn't understand yet. He knew, though, that he had good intuition and the angels had helpful spiritual information. It was clear that his journey would go a lot smoother if he would listen to both. Even if he didn't understand all of the words and ideas yet, he still had to trust that the angels knew more than he did about this land.

But he still had to walk the road himself.

"Why are there storms here, Orange?"

"Michael Thomas of Pure Intent, I will give you yet another true answer, but one that you will not understand." Orange stood up and walked back to the mouth of the cave. When he reached the opening, he turned and said, "When the human is not here, there are no storms."

Mike had no idea why that was so. He stood up to ask about the dark thing that he'd seen chasing him, but Orange was gone! He spoke to the empty space where the angel had been just a moment before. "Good-bye, again, my bright orange friend."

For the first time, there was an answer to his farewell! He clearly heard the voice of Orange in his head, soothing, loving, and wise. *"It is when you understand why we never say good-bye that you will know you are a part of our dimension."*

Mike was comforted by the angel's words, although Orange was right—these were answers that Mike didn't understand. Mike took off the armor and wrung out his socks. He stayed by the fire to get warm while his clothes dried on the rocks next to the dancing flames. He noticed that neither the armor nor the shield had a single scratch or dent as he carefully laid them next to his clothes. Sleep finally came.

The storm continued for a while but by the time Mike woke up, it was completely over. It was still the same day, but almost sundown.

Mike had slept the afternoon away and was now feeling full of energy. He got dressed, put his battle gear back on like Orange had shown him, lifted the map bag over his neck, and set out on the road again. It was so peaceful outside that Mike almost couldn't believe that a great storm had raged here only a few hours earlier. He looked behind him but didn't see any trace of the ugly thing that had been following him. He didn't feel any danger—in fact, he felt good!

Even though it was almost dark, Mike felt that the next house would be close by, and he was right—it was just over the next hill. Both of his hands were empty, and without his bulky gym bag, his battle gear didn't clink and clank. He felt so light that he almost forgot he had it on. His feet were good and solid on the road.

Mike started to believe that losing his precious things was right for his journey after all—and he made up his mind not to be upset about it anymore. He practiced looking at the baseball cards and pictures in his mind. He could remember it all! Mike still felt the love of his family and Bryan, and had all the feelings he was used to when he looked at the cards and pictures. Orange was right. Those feelings weren't in the pictures or the cards or the other keepsakes—they were in his mind. They would always be there, and no storm could take them away.

*   *   *

Far behind, a disgusting dark green shape was trying to snap out of a painful experience. Each time IT moved, the pain reminded it of the burn it had received. IT didn't know it, but that burn would never heal. IT was confused, but determined to stop Michael Thomas no matter what. It was life or death. IT knew that even if it had to die in battle, the time would soon come when Michael Thomas would look into a pair of burning red eyes, feel hot breath in his face, and know what it meant to be terribly afraid.

*   *   *   *   *   *

Chapter Seven
The Third House

Mike paused at the little footpath before he walked up to the third house. The sign on the lawn read "House of Biology." The whole house (and the sign) were all one glorious color, just like the other two houses had been. But this one was the beautiful bright green of St. Patrick's Day—the same shade as the grass and trees! The gentle light of the setting sun made it look very peaceful.

Mike knew that he was about to meet yet another grand angel who would become his friend. He thought about the first two houses he'd been to so far, where he was taught to be ready for whatever might happen on his journey. But Mike had the feeling that while at the Green House, he'd go through some more intense training. *After all that's happened so far, I'll bet that this house is really something.*

A huge green angel stepped out onto the porch, watched him walk up, and gave Mike the usual greeting: "Greetings, Michael Thomas of Pure Intent!"

This angel, whom Mike would automatically call Green, seemed even stronger and happier than the others. Blue and Orange were friendly and ready to laugh, but Green looked like he was always smiling.

The angel looked Mike up and down and grinned. "Nice sword!"

"Good evening to *you*, Green." Mike ignored the comment about the sword. *He probably just said that to make me feel better about carrying this thing.*

"No—I said it because it is true." Of course, the angel knew his thoughts. "Not all swords are as grand as the one you have. I know. I see lots of them."

"What's different about it, Green?"

"We named you for a reason, Michael. Your intent is indeed pure, and your heart actually rings with your quest. Your tools therefore show something that all of us angels can see. Please, come in."

Mike followed Green into the house, continuing the conversation. "Does that make me different?—Special?—Better?"

"It shows that it is possible for you to do some very wonderful things, Michael! Remember that as a human you have choice. We always look at you in that way—how quick you are to make choices, and how pure those choices are. That is what we call your *potential*. We see each human's energy potential."

"Potential for what?"

"Change!"

"Why?"

Green stopped and faced Mike. They'd just passed through several small green rooms and were now at the door to the room Mike would be staying in. The angel spoke softly and with a great deal of patience and honor for the little human he was standing before. "Why are you here, Michael Thomas?"

"To allow for my journey Home," Mike stated quickly and honestly.

"And what must you do to allow for that?" The angel was giving Mike a chance to think about what he'd learned on his journey so far, and say what he expected to learn from the rest of it.

"Travel on the road of seven houses?"

"And?" Green wanted more.

"Change to a being with a much higher vibration—think and act more like you?" Mike could only bashfully repeat what he remembered Orange had told him.

Green flashed a big smile. "Sometime soon, Michael Thomas of Pure Intent, you will really understand some of the words and ideas you're being asked about now. Did Orange tell you that?"

Mike was aware that Green knew those were Orange's words, not his. "Yes, he did. I really don't know what it all means yet."

"I know. So—back to the question. What are you doing about getting Home?"

"Changing!" Mike stated proudly.

"Why?" Now the question had come all the way back around, back to Mike's own question.

"I can't go Home until I change?"

"Exactly! The journey Home has several parts, my human friend. First, there is the intent—or *choice*—to go. Next is getting everything *ready* to go. Then comes learning about yourself, and understanding that you have to change yourself to get there. You already understand that. And finally, you must study how everything works here so that it will be easier for you to see things as we can. Opening that last door marked *Home* is like a graduation, Michael. There is nothing like it!"

This was the very first time an angel had talked about the last door and the end of the journey. Mike was very excited. "Tell me more about what to look forward to, Green." This is what Mike was really interested in—the final door—and what would happen when he opened that door.

"When you first asked, you said it yourself."

"When was that?"

"When you first asked for this journey, Michael."

Mike suddenly remembered the conversation that had started all this, with the great faceless angel in white, when he was asked to tell what he thought Home was. "You know about that?" Mike was surprised.

"We are all part of the same family, Michael." Green floated into the room where Mike was to stay. It was much the same as the rooms he'd stayed in while at other houses along his journey, and it looked cozy and comfortable. He smelled the food that was prepared for him in the next room.

"There are also clothes this time, Michael." The angel pointed toward the closet.

Mike suddenly thought about what a sight he must be, with blood and dried mud on his ragged shirt and pants that had been torn by the storm. He opened the closet. There certainly were clothes! He saw fine outfits for traveling and a grand green robe. Mike turned to ask Green how they knew his size, but Green had disappeared. Mike smiled and said out loud, knowing Green would hear him, "Good night, my green angelic friend. See you in the morning."

Mike was very hungry and tired, and he ate and slept soundly that night until about 5 A.M., when he had a nightmare. In his dream, he saw the horrible thing coming closer to him when he was flat on the ground in the storm, fighting for his life. This thing wanted to kill him, and he was terrified. He woke right up, sweating all over. Green was standing by the bed!

"Ready, Michael?"

"Do you guys ever sleep?" asked Mike, rubbing his eyes.

"Of course not."

"The sun isn't even up yet!" Mike still felt tired. The terrible nightmare had disrupted his sleep.

"Get used to it in the House of Biology, Michael Thomas." Green continued to stand there. "Biology means a study of the human body. I'll be here each morning at 5:30 to start the lessons. By the time we are finished, you will understand all about your body's energy and what happens when you sleep—and when you have bad dreams."

"You know about my dreams?" Mike was amazed.

"Michael, you still don't understand how we are all connected to you. We know all about you, and we honor your process greatly!" Green took a few steps back from the bed and motioned for Mike to get ready and go with him.

Mike did as he was asked and went into the next room to enjoy his breakfast. Green was right by his side and watched everything he ate but said nothing. This was the first time an angelic teacher had paid this kind of attention to him. Something was different.

After the meal, Green led Mike to a special teaching room. The other houses had been huge, with large rooms and high ceilings. In this one, all the rooms were small, and there was only one teaching room. Green started right in. "Michael Thomas of Pure Intent—point to your spiritual understanding."

"I don't understand."

"Where is your pure intent? Where is your love? Where is that part of you that knows God?" Green was serious, and continued, "Go ahead. Point to that part of your biology—your body—that has all of that."

Mike didn't have to think very hard about this. Now he understood that Green, who wasn't human, wanted him to show where in his body all that stuff was. "Some is here." Mike pointed to his forehead. "And some is here." Mike put the palm of his hand over his heart.

"Wrong!" Green's booming voice surprised Mike. "Let me tell you a joke, Michael Thomas. Then you may try again."

Very funny. Here Mike was, talking to a green angel in a land that didn't exist before—and the angel was about to tell him a joke! Who'd ever believe this? Was this a great place or what?

"Once there was a man who felt very wise," Green began. "When the man felt he was wise enough to continue his journey, he hailed a taxi." Green smiled big and stopped, looking for Mike to be surprised that an angel knew about taxis. But Mike just pretended that it was no big deal and kept the smile off his lips. Green continued anyway.

"When the taxi stopped, the man stuck his head in the window and said to the driver, 'I'm ready. Let's go!' The driver, doing just what the man asked him to, stepped on the gas to go where the man wanted—with only the man's head in the car!" Green really was very funny, and he looked at Mike to see what he thought of his story so far.

Mike still looked right back at Green. "And?" Mike asked.

Green delivered the punch line. "Blessed is the man who puts his whole body into the taxi before saying that he is ready to go!" Green beamed. He was very proud of himself. He knew he was a good storyteller even though Mike had managed to keep a straight face.

"Very funny." Mike tried hard not to laugh out loud at this very funny angel. "So what exactly does your joke mean, Green?"

"Michael Thomas of Pure Intent, each and every cell of your body knows about God, so it is possible for each cell to have wisdom and love, and each one can change. Here, let me show you." With that, he did something that shocked Mike. With a move like lightning, Green stomped on Mike's toe!

"OW!" Green had turned on him! "What's THAT all about?" Mike's toe was screaming with pain. He forgot he was talking to an angel and yelled, "Are you out of your mind, man!" He grabbed his foot and hopped all around, trying to make the pain go away somehow. His toe turned red, then black. "That hurt a lot! I think you broke it!"

"What hurts, Michael?" Green asked as he watched Mike hop around in pain.

"My TOE, you slime-colored bully!" Mike yelled back angrily.

But Green's feelings weren't hurt by what Mike had said to him, and he approached Mike.

"Stay away!" Mike held out his hands to keep Green away. "I don't want any more of what you think is angel foot therapy. Don't come any closer!"

"What hurts, Michael?" Green asked again patiently. "It's not your toe."

"It's not?" More angel trickery. Mike sat on the floor, blowing on his foot, trying not to tip over. "Then tell me, your Holy Greenness. What is it that hurts?"

"WE do, Michael. Each and every cell in your body is feeling your hurt right now. Say it, Michael. *We hurt.*"

"We hurt," he repeated with no feeling at all.

"Do you give permission for a healing?"

"Yes, I sure do." Mike was interested now.

"State your permission."

"I give you permission to heal my toe."

"WRONG!"

Mike didn't need a map to get this one right. He tried again. "I give you permission to heal . . . WE—er—I mean, US."

Green still wasn't satisfied.

"Michael, give permission for the healing to happen, don't give *me* permission to do it."

Mike thought about this and said it again a bit differently. "I give permission for this healing. *We* hurt, and *we* will all be better with the healing."

"And so it is!" shouted Green excitedly, clapping his hands. "You are correct, Michael Thomas of Pure Intent! You have just healed your toe!"

Almost immediately, Mike's toe stopped throbbing. It turned a healthy pink again, and his whole body felt better. The pain was gone.

Green came closer, and this time Mike didn't ask him to stop. "Michael, do you know what just happened?" Green asked gently.

"I think I do, but I need you to explain anyway." Mike was exhausted.

"I'll never again cause you pain, my dear human friend. I promise. From now on, you'll learn from experiences other than pain. What you just learned was that the pain of the one part affects all of the parts. It happened to your whole body. You are really tired now, right? If this had happened only to your toe, then why would your whole body feel it? And why were you angry? Did your toe shout at me? No. Your entire *body* shouted at me! Your toe knew of the pain, but all of you was involved. The toe was where the problem was, but I guarantee that all the cells knew about it. The same is true of joy, pleasure, all deep feelings. Each cell feels everything and knows about all the rest of the cells." Green paused so that Mike could see how important this was. "So it is with spiritual learning and a Godly journey."

"Then where exactly is the part of me that knows God, Green?" Mike wanted a straight answer this time—no jokes or toe-stompings.

"It is the same in each cell of your body, Michael Thomas. Each cell absolutely knows about the other cells. Each one has a part in the vibration of the whole human." Green was quiet for a moment, then turned and sat down in front of Mike. "During your time here, you will learn how vibrations are increased. Before we can start, you must know that you are a group of cells that all know everything—not just a bunch of pieces."

"I think I understand that."

"Good." Green smiled his great big smile and got up. "Are you ready?"

Still smarting from the toe experience, Mike felt himself being raised from the floor. "Yes, sir, I am."

During the next few hours, Mike learned what to eat, how to have energy, and how to exercise. There seemed to be so much great information about everything! All through the lessons, Green made sure Mike understood the *we* of his being. Mike was starting to feel as if he wasn't allowed to have parts, and Green agreed.

Mike slept very well that night—no more nightmares. Green woke him promptly at 5:30 and went with him to breakfast. This time Green talked about each type of food that Mike was eating. Mike chewed away, trying to remember everything that Green was saying.

During the next few days, Mike began an exercise program. On certain days, Green made him put on his battle gear again so that he wouldn't forget what it felt like. Those were the days Mike enjoyed most. He didn't realize how much he missed his sword, shield, and armor until he put them on and was amazed by how well they fit.

Green taught Mike about food, plants, herbs, and how the body kept itself in balance naturally. It was amazing how the cells worked together, as if they knew something he didn't.

Green told Mike that each organ and cell was arranged in a certain way magnetically. The cells all knew this, and by themselves worked to keep everything balanced and in good working order. When in balance, each cell could make itself well perfectly, and the body constantly healed itself.

Mike had to then ask Green a question. "It seems that my cells—I mean, *we*—are very smart when it comes to balancing the body. Why don't I seem to know what's going on? Is there something I can do to help the body do all this? Where do I, as Mike, fit into all this?"

"Funny you should ask, Michael Thomas of Pure Intent! Your body only needs you to honor it by taking care of it. Eat good food and protect it from too much sun or cold, and your body will do the rest. So far, you have learned how to make it comfortable, feed it properly, and give it some exercise. Your body is happy and busy without your doing anything else. Now, it is time for you to understand the test of your spirit, for you have something to give your body that it could never do for itself. Do you know what that is?"

Mike thought that he did. "Yes, I do, Green." Mike was feeling stronger and healthier than he had in a long time. "It's time for me to make a choice," Mike blurted out.

Green almost exploded with happiness. He was like a loving father and a great teacher. "Never before has a human understood this in such a short time!"

Mike had finally said something right. And he couldn't believe Green's reaction. The angel shot around the room, floating all around and changing his shape. He wasn't afraid because he realized that Green was showing off especially for him.

When Green finally calmed down, he stood again in front of Mike. He looked like his green angelic self but was still wide-eyed with pride and happiness. "Michael Thomas of Pure Intent, what is your choice?"

"I choose to use the new tools and gifts of Spirit and increase my vibration." Again, Mike knew he'd said something right.

Green backed up a few steps as if to give Mike and his increased wisdom room to swell all around him. He was obviously very impressed. "So it shall be this very day, Michael Thomas! You are right. Only your spirit, not your cells, can actually use the piece of God you carry with you that has the power to choose more spiritual knowledge. Even so, each cell will know that you gave permission. Just like when your toe hurt, your spirit knew it. So it is that when you ask for a higher vibration, your toe will know it. The we-ness of you is so happy right now, Michael. We all know what you've given intent for. It's time you went to bed and got some rest."

It had been a grand day, and Mike was starting to feel that he was understanding more of these spiritual things. He'd done some pretty special things.

As they walked together, Green spoke. He said that Mike had given intent for a spiritual quest, a choice to have more spiritual knowledge that would take him to a higher vibration. This quest was the first of many that Mike would have to ask for. And when it was time to take the next step, Green told Mike that his body would have to be balanced and he'd have to give permission.

Green was proud of Mike and was treating him with even more respect than usual. When they reached the door to Mike's room, Green faced him, saying, "Michael Thomas of Pure Intent, normally I just disappear now and come back in the morning. I am here to tell you that I love you dearly. A change in vibration does things to you that you must learn about and get used to. From here on, you will control how fast everything happens. Any hurt you feel will be from you. Nothing will ever be the same for you. This night you go to sleep as one kind of human, but tomorrow you'll be another—with everything the new vibration will bring."

Green looked at Mike a very long time, and Mike felt the amazing honor Green was showing him, but wanted Green to explain more. *What's different? What will I know tomorrow? What's tomorrow's lesson? Tell me now!*

Mike didn't ask any of these questions out loud, and Green pretended he couldn't hear Mike. Instead, Green slowly backed away—he didn't just disappear as he had every other night. Something was changing, and Mike had a funny feeling about it all. He spoke out loud to the walls: "I guess I have to expect more changes as I get closer to that final door to Home."

Mike sat on the bed. "Maybe I'll even become an angel before I get there. I might even turn a special color!" Mike laughed at that thought, and as before, he expected to hear a remark from one of the ever-listening angels. But there was only silence. Something inside him was already starting to change. His stomach was a bit queasy and he was having chills. He had to get to bed.

Mike didn't sleep well that night. He wished it was already time to get up. He wished he was back with Green, learning the lessons that would take him Home. But instead, each time he fell asleep, he had the same bad dream. IT was there, glaring at him, and each time the gross thing caught him, IT destroyed him! IT tore him to shreds and threw him far and wide. He woke himself up screaming, in a pool of sweat and fear. Then there would be only the deepest silence filling the room.

When Mike dropped off to sleep again, the dream would come back. How many times could he be killed? Five? Six? It seemed like it would never end. He was killed over and over, each time a bit differently. And each time, his dream seemed more real.

Finally, he couldn't take it anymore and started crying. He was so scared and sad that he was crying his whole heart and soul into the pillow! He didn't even cry this hard when Bryan moved away! He cried loudly, then he started wailing, and then he really lost control.

Mike felt sorry for himself. He cried for lost friendship, for things he thought had been taken away from him, and things he thought he'd missed out on. He felt that IT had killed him, and Mike cried for his own death. He shook with each tear and couldn't stop thinking about all of the things he had to be sad about.

Mike wore himself out crying and fell into a deep sleep for a few hours. When he finally woke up, he had the feeling that something was wrong. It was almost light outside. *Where is Green? Why did he let me sleep so late?* Mike got up and instantly felt a pain in his stomach from last night's crying. He held himself.

"Boy, do *we* hurt!" he heard himself say to his body.

He put on his green robe and went into the room where he usually ate his meals. No food. *What gives?* He began to search for Green. He noticed that the rooms now looked like they were an ugly brownish green—or was that just the light? Speaking of light, it seemed to be getting dimmer. *What's happening here?* Mike expected the angel to answer his thoughts, but there was no response.

"Green, where are you?" Mike spoke out loud, but still there was no answer.

Mike walked through the house but couldn't find the angel anywhere. Finally, hungry and tired, he sat down alone in the room where Green taught him his lessons. He was puzzled and was starting to feel depressed. He hadn't felt this bad since before he set off on his journey.

"What's happening?" Mike wondered out loud. "Where is everyone? Blue? Orange? Green? Hey guys, I need you!"

He was answered only by silence.

Mike realized that his depression was already taking over. It wouldn't be long before he was in that same hole where he didn't care about anything or anyone. He just couldn't let that happen.

"Okay, guys, if you won't help me, then I'll do it the HARD way!" Whatever that meant. Mike was trying to get some kind of reaction from the angels. He knew they were out there listening and watching.

He went back to the bedroom and looked around. When he opened the closet, he remembered the map! Maybe it would give him a clue. It always did when something was wrong in this odd land where things were so current. Mike found it easily and unrolled it.

He wasn't ready for what he saw there. He didn't want to believe it and put the map away as if he were in a trance. He got back into bed, robe and all, and pulled the covers up around his head. It was already the afternoon, but Mike didn't care. He stared into the covers.

Instead of the trusty *"You Are Here"* dot, there was only a dark black smudge, nothing more. There were no markings on the map at all! It was dead!

Had IT invaded the house and actually killed Mike during the night? Had he been dreaming, or were his dreams all real? Had IT also killed the angels? What was going on here? Mike tried to fight his deep black sadness. He had to figure this all out. He stretched his mind, trying to remember the least little thing Green might have said that would explain this.

Then, through the black haze in his mind, Mike remembered Green telling him: *"Any pain from now on will be from you. Nothing will ever be the same; I love you dearly."* Had this been Green's way of saying good-bye? Mike remembered again what the great white one had said at the beginning: *"Not everything is as it seems . . ."*

Things looked pretty bad, but Mike just had to hang on. He knew God wouldn't leave him in a fix like this, that this had to be a trick or a test.

Then he did the only thing he could think of. He got up and put on his armor. It didn't feel good. It was heavier than he remembered, and the sword felt stupid. He didn't care. He wore it with pride and spoke out loud, "Nothing will break my spirit! I claim victory over my sadness!"

Nothing. Silence. Empty words. No feeling of love or honor, or that anyone or anything cared about him. This land was completely empty. Michael Thomas was the only one there.

He was trying to stay calm. This was too weird. But Mike wouldn't give up! He went to the lesson room and sat in his usual place in full battle dress. He stayed there until the sun went down, waiting and watching in the deep quiet of a land with no sound. Even then, he continued to sit there, alert and waiting. He didn't know what would happen, but he wouldn't give in to the dark sadness. He'd fought it many times in his old life, and he sure wasn't about to give in to it here in this angel land.

Finally, Mike fell asleep in the dark room. His sleep wasn't disturbed by bad dreams this time. Everything was starting to settle down—with his patience and determination, Mike was making everything around him calm and peaceful. He'd already received the gifts and tools to do this, and his understanding was beginning to show. As he slept, his sword gently sang to itself. His shield glowed a bit, and his armor kept him warm—all feeling the new vibration of the precious human who owned them.

But Mike didn't know any of this. All the cells in his body were being changed, and that change was almost complete. Michael Thomas slept very well indeed.

$$* \quad * \quad *$$

Things were different when Mike woke up the next morning. He was still in the chair that he'd slept in all night, but the room was brighter and more cheerful somehow. He got up and tested his mind. Odd that his first thought was to see if he was okay, not to see if he was still alone. The dark sadness was gone! Mike was still in his battle gear, but it felt so light and natural that he didn't even notice he had it on. He quickly walked over to the dining room, hoping that he wouldn't have to go hungry again today. Halfway there, the wonderful smells of a fine breakfast greeted him. Everything was going to be all right again.

Mike ate like he had never eaten before. He was starving. He felt so good and so happy that he started singing out loud—with his mouth full! "Mom should see me now!" Mike said, a bit of egg falling off the corner of his mouth. "She'd be pretty ashamed at my bad manners."

"She's actually very proud of you, Mike." Green was standing at the door. "We all are."

Mike stood up out of respect for his green friend. He was overjoyed to see the angel.

"Green!" Mike yelled in delight. "I wondered if I'd lost you. Please, come sit down with me!" Mike sat back down and continued eating.

The large angel went to the table and sat down, but waited for Mike to speak first. He knew that his little friend would have many questions about yesterday but wanted to see how long it would take him to ask. There was silence while Mike continued eating and humming at the same time, smiling foolishly and looking at Green with sparkling eyes.

Green took it all in, looking closely at Michael's body, noticing the full battle dress. He couldn't keep quiet any longer. "Nice sword," said the green one with a wise smile.

Mike burst out laughing at the remark, remembering that this was what Green had first said to him when he'd come to this house. Food went everywhere, and the great green one started laughing, too. They hugged, a warm and happy hug. It was the first time that Mike had been allowed to touch any of the angels, but he knew inside that it was okay. They couldn't stop laughing. Mike found himself actually dancing with the great green angel to the music of his very soul, stomping on bagels and muffins that got knocked off the table in the ruckus. He saw the pieces of blueberry muffin stuck between his toes, and he laughed even more. The room was a mess, but he didn't care.

It was quite a celebration. Mike sat down, trying to catch his breath. He finally spoke to Green, who stood before him. "I knew you'd come back, you know."

"How did you know?"

"Because you told me you loved me."

"That I do." Green flashed another proud smile.

Mike took another bite of the food left on the table. "You know, Green, I last felt this happy at my Grandma's house. But she died when I was six. I like to think that she can still see me. Can she?" This meant a lot to him.

"I can see by this first question how much you've learned in this land, Michael Thomas of Pure Intent. Sometimes we angels here bet on which question will be asked first after a human spends a long night like you have, going through the change. The one that's normally asked, you've not yet asked me. We've been together again in this room for some time—yet you've still not asked it. Instead, you ask about your Grandma. Truly, I stand before a special human being!"

Mike wasn't sure, but he thought Green was getting emotional—if that was possible for an angel. It was a minute before Green spoke again.

"Yes, Michael Thomas, your Grandma can see you, and she is very proud." Green waited for more questions.

"I think I know what yesterday was all about."

Green tilted his head to one side. "Really? Tell me, then. I'm all ears." Usually after the long sad and lonely night, Green had to explain where everyone had gone to and why it was necessary to go through all that pain and sadness.

"I've changed, Green, just like you said I would. I feel different. I feel . . . *we* feel more powerful. I have a stronger feeling about you, Green, that I didn't have before. Instead of just being my wonderful teacher, now you feel more like—" Mike couldn't come up with the right words. Green interrupted him.

"Family?"

"Yes!" Mike quickly agreed. He wanted to think about this some more, but continued. "What happened yesterday—I thought it was a test, but it wasn't." Green continued to listen, letting Mike tell his ideas of what had happened. "I know that you'll explain it better to me later, but I think I know the *why*."

Mike said it slowly and carefully, as a teacher would. "Green, every cell in my body felt strange and far away from this place. It was like I turned off a switch and died. There was no safe feeling anywhere; I couldn't even think of a good reason to continue on my journey. Somehow, I was between my old self and my new self. And when I looked at the map and saw only the big black smudge, that's when I realized what was happening. I was scared at first, but the smudge was a kind of signal to my mind, and then I understood. I was in the middle of changing to my new vibratory level, just like we'd talked about. And can you believe it? I'm finally starting to get used to some of these big words."

Green was impressed. Never before had a student in the Green House been so right about how it was to change to a new vibration. It usually took a long time to explain. Green knew that he sat before a truly special human, this young Michael Thomas. He was proud of his student and loved him even more.

"The map died, too, Green! I was nowhere; then, I knew what was happening. So I could move on, with pure intent to go Home, I had to receive this special gift of higher vibration. It felt like being born all over again. I knew that if I stayed calm somehow, everything would turn out okay. I kept remembering that you loved me, Green. It's the only thing that worked. When I thought about you, then I could concentrate on why I was here." Mike looked at Green and smiled. He tried to hide the tears starting in his eyes. "Am I right?"

"There's almost nothing I can add, Michael Thomas of Pure Intent." Green stood up because what he was going to say next was very important. "I tell you this: When you were thinking about how much I loved you, it wasn't just me. I am just one of many, Michael. When you speak to me, you are speaking to the whole group. You are part of it, too, but you don't yet feel it like I do. As you change and vibrate even higher, you will understand these things more easily. When you felt the love of the one you call Green, you were also feeling the love of Blue, Orange, and even your Grandma—and all the ones you are going to meet down the road. You don't know them yet, but they already know you. We are all one, Michael, and you felt it at the moment you needed it most. Your intuition won! What a gift you already have!"

Mike knew there was more, so he kept quiet, waiting for Green to gather his thoughts.

"Everything you said is correct, my wise little friend. When moving to a higher level, the lessons are hard and you have to *make* it happen. It is a time when all of us in the group must step back and let you change. We can't do anything for you during this time because our energy is too strong and would change the way your lessons go. You have to handle this yourself, the way *you* choose to do it. You have the power and the tools and will be able to move right through the lessons. You missed your Grandma, Michael. You felt strange and lost during the short time that you had to be by yourself. The only thing that kept you going was Love, and I, as a teacher in this house, could never have given you that answer. You found it in the blackness for yourself. I am proud that you were able to do so." Green paused again to let the compliment sink in. "Any other questions?"

"Will it happen again?"

"Yes, it will; each time you have learned enough to change to a new vibratory level."

"What can I do to make the next time easier?"

Green faced Mike and spoke seriously. "Know it for what it is and get busy with other things. Don't sit around and feel sorry for yourself, and remember that it will last only a short time. Give thanks for the gift of change and honor it in the middle of all the blackness! Do exactly as you did, Michael Thomas of Pure Intent—feel the love behind the gift!"

Mike felt like he understood. He had no more questions.

✳ ✳ ✳

The lessons began again. Because of Mike's new vibratory rate, there was even more for Green to teach him. He learned to pay attention to his body's little hints if something was wrong. Green explained how different sleeping and eating would be for each new vibratory change. There was so much to remember!

The last day in the Green House came fast.

"I sure hope I remember all this later!" Mike thought aloud.

Green laughed and said, "Michael, you can be sure that you'll remember. It may seem that you are learning things you won't need since you are going Home. But you are going to have to trust me and know that you will need every bit of it.

And you will remember when you need to. If you think of your body as sacred, then you will be able to honor it even more than you do now."

Mike knew Green was right. Now all the parts of his body, large or small, could be part of the *we* with more respect!

The next day, it was time to go. Mike dressed in the new green road clothes. What he'd learned in this house had really gotten his attention. As he stood on the doorstep of the Green House in the warm sun next to Green, he didn't know what to say.

He felt good. His battle gear looked great over his new clothes, and the material felt good on his body. Everything fit so well, and he wondered how whoever made the clothes could have known his new size—he'd done some growing during the past few weeks.

Green looked him over carefully, his eyes resting on Mike's sword for a minute, and was about to say something.

Mike saw this and said quickly, "I know, I know—nice sword!"

It was Green's turn to burst out laughing. "You took the words right out of my angel mouth." The two stood quietly in the warm sunlight.

"Promise me that I'll see you again, Green."

"I promise, Michael," Green said right away.

"Don't you have a question for me?" Mike prompted Green for the last question before he had to get back on the road.

"I sure do, and you know what it is." Green looked hard at Michael Thomas. "Do you wish to answer it before I ask?"

"Yes, I do," he said like he was about to start a big speech. "I love God with all my heart. My intent is pure, and my body is part of the Spirit of all of you. I'm much closer to your vibration, and I feel more determined, more sacred, and that I belong here. I'm on my way Home."

There was nothing Green could say.

The angels in the other houses before had simply gone inside without saying good-bye. But this time, it was Mike who left without saying good-bye. He walked down the path very sure of himself, heading north toward the hills where he knew the next house would be.

Green stayed on the porch until Mike disappeared down the road. Then he said out loud, "Michael Thomas of Pure Intent, if you make it through the next house, you are indeed the warrior that I think you are." Green stayed on the porch, waiting.

It wasn't long before a disgusting, ugly green creature slipped past the house on its dark mission, following Mike and looking right at Green as he passed.

The angel said nothing. Green knew all about IT. Green also knew that Michael would soon find out about IT. He smiled at the idea. *What a meeting that will be!* the angel thought. Then, he turned and went back into the Green House.

✳ ✳ ✳ ✳ ✳ ✳

Chapter Eight
The Fourth House

Mike was feeling better than ever, and he walked along without any worries. His new sense of power, specially made clothes, and magnificent battle gear fit perfectly and seemed to belong on the journey. He finally felt comfortable on the path and was beginning to recognize the smell and look of things. Memories of his old life were beginning to slip away—*this* was starting to feel more like home to him. Mike sensed that there was something familiar about this land, as if he remembered it from somewhere. But he knew he'd never been there before.

Mike had learned a lot in the green House of Biology, and he smiled as he thought about Green. He knew he'd truly moved to a new level while he was there. He'd been through only three of the houses so far and wondered what lessons waited for him in the next four.

There was a sound behind him!

Like lightning, Mike spun around to defend himself—he didn't even have to think about it first. He leaned forward, his hand tight around the big handle of his fine Sword of Truth. Was it his imagination, or was the handle vibrating? His ears were ringing, and he was listening hard for any sound as he stood like a statue waiting to spring into some unknown but perfect action.

Nothing.

It could have been the wind, but then Mike noticed that no leaves were moving in the trees by the road. Using only his eyes, keeping the rest of his body perfectly still, he scanned the area. How sharp his eyes were in this place! He didn't remember being able to see so well before! It was almost as if someone had turned on a bright light.

Mike studied every large rock and cliff in sight.

Nothing.

He began to understand that even though he was comfortable in this new land, it was still a dangerous place for him. His dark stalker might still be out there. He had to be careful. But Mike wasn't scared. He stayed very still, watching everything, straining his eyes, ears, and heart for even the smallest clue that there might be danger.

Even with his sharper eyes and ears, Mike couldn't see or hear anything unusual. But he was discovering something new about himself. He could *feel* that something was out there. He had a bad feeling in his soul—a feeling of danger and a warning that he could be killed.

After a few minutes, he decided it was safe to continue walking along the sunny road, but he did keep his eyes darting left and right so he could spot anything unusual. *What's following me? In a land so full of love and spiritual lessons, how could there be such a dark thing in it? And why does IT want me? Why didn't the angels want to talk about IT?*

It was a great mystery indeed. Mike felt as if he'd been warned, and he wasn't about to let this evil thing sneak up on him again. He stayed ready for action.

The sun would be going down soon, and Mike hadn't come to the next house yet. He stopped and turned to look back down the road. Nothing moved, and he didn't hear anything. He took out his map and was thankful to see that it worked again. The *"You Are Here"* dot was right in the middle, just as before. On the edge of the small area around the dot was the next house. Mike smiled, put his map away, and started walking again.

The journey to the next house took almost a full day. Mike realized that the houses were just far enough away from each other so that if he walked quickly, he could get from one to another without having to spend the night outside in the dark. He was glad of that. He was tired and knew that it wasn't just from the walk—he'd been watching for IT all day.

In that mysterious time just before the sun goes down, when everything seems to turn one warm color, Mike rounded the bend in the road to the next house. Although everything around it was lit by the orange and red light of the passing day, the little house softly glowed its own pure violet color. Mike stopped and just stared with his mouth open. Never had he seen such an incredible color! The violet was intense, soothing, and powerful all at the same time. The house had the look of a beautiful violet lamp, glowing from inside. He walked on, remembering that to stop for too long wasn't smart, even though he was close to the violet house.

When the house's angel appeared at the door to greet him, Mike couldn't speak! The angel was so beautiful! Mike almost felt that he should kneel in respect! What was happening? Had his eyes changed so much that he could see more color? He stood in wonder at the sight, and then he heard the voice—oh, wow, what a voice! Silky smooth and soothing, it was the voice of a lady!

"Greetings, Michael Thomas of Pure Intent." The wonderful voice flowed through him. "We've been waiting for you."

Mike was mesmerized and couldn't make his mouth work. He couldn't even think. And he'd stopped breathing.

Violet smiled and continued. "I'm no more a woman than Green was, Michael. Angels aren't women *or* men, but they have features of *both*. The way I look and speak will make you more comfortable in this house."

None of this made any sense to Mike. He could breathe now but still couldn't talk. He didn't know what to say to such a gorgeous creature. Finally, he croaked out like a frog, "You're really something!" *What a stupid thing to say to such a beautiful angel!* Mike felt like a goofy little boy.

Mike realized that the beautiful angel had the voice and face of a lady, but there wasn't any difference between her body and the bodies of the other angels. They all wore flowing robes the color of their houses. All of them were huge—but this face! Violet definitely had a lady's face. It was soft and gentle and more beautiful than any saint in the wonderful windows at church. Mike sighed and tried again.

"Please forgive me, uh . . . Violet." Mike struggled with his manners. "I didn't expect—I mean, I didn't know that you would look like such a beautiful lady to me."

Mike was immediately sorry he'd opened his mouth again. How stupid that was! Of course this angel could look like a lady! Why not? It just caught him by surprise, that's all. Violet just stood there. He tried again.

"What I mean is . . . none of the other angels so far . . . they seemed to be guys . . . men." Mike wanted to start this all over. What was the matter with him? This was no proper greeting for such an angel. He sighed and finally decided to just keep quiet.

Violet smiled at Mike. "I understand fully, Michael Thomas."

It was weird, but Violet kind of reminded him of his mom. He hadn't seen his mom in such a long time. All he wanted to do was snuggle up in Violet's arms and be held like a baby. Then he was embarrassed, remembering that Violet would know his thoughts.

"You will get used to it very soon, Michael. There are reasons why I look this way to you. It is not this way with all those who travel this road, but for you it is different."

Mike got the idea. Violet looked and acted this way just for him, but why did he need to see such a beautiful, motherly angel?

"Because you earned it! Not everything here is just for lessons, Michael. Much of it is a gift because you have done so well so far. You have only been through three houses, and you are already one of the most special humans ever to join us here."

Mike took all that in, but before he could speak again, Violet did something that Mike would never forget.

"Michael Thomas of Pure Intent," she said softly, "please take off your shoes."

Mike did as he was asked. He noticed a spot by the door for one pair of shoes, so he put his there. They fit perfectly.

"Michael, do you know why I have asked this?"

He thought about it. "Because it's sacred ground inside?" He remembered the story of Moses and the burning bush, and how the ground up on the mountain was holy.

"If that were the reason, then why did you not have to do so at the other houses?"

Mike continued to think about it. He tried again. "Because you're a very special angel?"

Violet thought this was funny and smiled. But Mike was confused and knew he still hadn't given the right answer.

"Please come inside," Violet said as she turned and entered the house.

Mike followed her, but he felt as if they hadn't finished their conversation. He called as he followed, "Violet, tell me. Why *did* you ask me to take off my shoes?"

"You will tell me, Michael, before you leave this place."

Mike didn't like it when the angels made him wait for answers, especially when he was expected to somehow figure it out for himself. *Too much work,* Mike thought.

"That is why you are here," said Violet as she led him farther into the house. Mike reminded himself to watch his thoughts.

The Violet House was very plain—not like its angel at all. In fact, he had been so surprised at how Violet looked that he forgot to look at the sign out front so he'd know the name of the house. "Violet, what's the name of this house?"

Violet stopped, turned, and faced Mike. "It is the House of Responsibility, Michael Thomas."

Mike immediately knew there was trouble ahead. "Oh," he said very quietly.

Violet had expected him to say more than that. She turned and continued the tour.

Mike was upset when he heard the name of the house. He let his mind go, dreaming up crazy scenes of what might take place here. *Responsibility* had always been an ugly word. His parents used it many times, and it never meant any good for him. He also heard the same word at school, when his teacher let him know how unhappy she was about something he did.

Violet led him through a bunch of hallways on the way to Mike's rooms.

"What's in there?" Mike asked as they came to a set of large double doors.

"The theater," said Violet, never missing a step.

A theater? Mike's thoughts were racing as he continued to follow Violet. *What's a theater doing in an angel house? Will there be a play? Maybe I'll watch a movie!* Mike thought about how funny it would be if tomorrow he and Violet went to a movie together. He almost laughed out loud. Violet, knowing exactly what Mike was thinking, thought it was very funny, too—but for other reasons.

Finally, they arrived. The dining room and bedroom looked like those in the other houses. In the closet, there were beautiful violet clothes and slippers made especially for Mike to wear while he was visiting the Violet House. He smelled food.

Knowing that Mike was hungry from his journey, Violet led him to the dining room, where many wonderful dishes were spread out on the table. *How do the angels always know exactly when I'm going to get here? And I've still never seen a single cook or clean-up person.* Mike remembered the mess he and Green had left after their fun, and how the blueberries had stained his toes for days. Like fairies, whoever prepared the food and cleaned up the mess did so without ever being seen. What a place!

Mike expected to turn and see that Violet had left the room, as the other angels always did. But she was still there.

"Is there anything else you need, Michael?" Violet was indeed a beautiful creature. She still seemed motherly to Mike, which made him feel quite content.

"No, thank you." Mike bowed.

"In the morning, we shall begin. Good night, Michael Thomas of Pure Intent." With this, Violet left the room.

This angel was very polite! Green had stayed on the porch as Mike left the House of Biology, but none of the angels had wished him a good night. Mike shrugged, and after he had set down his shield and sword, he made his way to the next room for dinner.

Mike ate, got ready for bed, and immediately fell fast asleep. He felt safe, warm, and loved. The next day would be the start of another adventure. He dreamed about Bryan and his parents, and it felt good.

＊　＊　＊

Outside the house, IT found a perfect spot to watch from. Deep in thought, and mad as a hornet, IT couldn't believe how much that little human had changed when he left the Green House! He was so much more powerful now. He had those blasted weapons, and with the sharp eyes and ears of a warrior, he also had no fear! IT growled in rage that it had failed in the storm to get rid of Michael once and for all.

IT developed a new plan. IT realized that Michael would always follow the road. Michael had no choice, since he didn't know where the next house would be. Therefore, IT decided, the answer was to go ahead of Michael and wait for him to step into the trap. If IT ever smiled, IT was doing so now. IT went to sleep and dreamed of putting a stop to the journey of Michael Thomas of Pure Intent.

＊　＊　＊

Mike topped off his usual outstanding breakfast with a blueberry muffin. With each bite, he was reminded of the wild dance he and Green had done and how gross blueberry muffins feel when they're smashed between your toes. He didn't know what

the day would bring, but he hurried from the breakfast room anyway, wanting to be ready when Violet came for him.

He had just finished putting on his violet clothes when he
heard a knock at the door. *A knock? Since when did any angel knock?*

"Please come in." Mike answered. Violet seemed to float in.

Mike smiled at her. "Please thank whoever made me such a
fine human breakfast."

"You are welcome."

"Was it you?"

"It was all of us. We are all together."

"I've heard that before. Someday I'll understand it. Until
then, I thank all of you very much."

"Are you ready, Michael?"

"Yes . . . I am."

Violet turned and led the way back to the theater they'd
passed the day before. This time the big doors were open, and
Mike followed her in. What a beautiful violet-colored movie theater! Mike stopped, not believing his eyes.

In front of them was a giant wraparound movie screen. A
modern film projector stood in the back of the room, with reel
after reel of film stacked in giant metal cans.

"And now, Michael Thomas, we are going to watch movies
together."

"I don't believe it! An angel showing movies. This is some kind
of joke, isn't it?"

With that, Violet stopped smiling and became serious.

"Far from it, Michael. Far from it. Please take your seat in the
front row."

Violet went to the back of the room, where she began warm-
ing up the machinery. Mike was still confused. *Movie theaters don't
belong in angel houses. This is too strange!* But he went to a seat
in the middle of the front row as he was told. This theater wasn't

like the ones he was used to—the front row wasn't actually in the front . . . it was in the middle of the room. He noticed something else odd. The middle chair in the front row was padded and soft, but the others weren't, as if no one was expected to sit in them. Mike sat down in the comfy violet seat and faced the giant white screen.

"What are we going to see, Violet?" Mike was getting a bit nervous about this.

"Home movies, Michael, home movies." She continued to get the first reel ready, not looking up. Mike didn't like the sound of that answer at all. And there was that strange feeling in his stomach again! It was his new intuition—now he knew why it was called a "gut feeling." It was working overtime, warning him of something unpleasant. He thought about jokingly asking Violet for some popcorn, but he didn't get the chance. The lights dimmed just like at any other theater; he heard the clatter of the projector, and the movie started. Mike's eyes were glued to the screen, and his heart was in his throat from the very first minute.

That first film, as he'd see with all the others, was so much more real than any movie he'd ever seen. It seemed as if the action was really happening there in front of him! The big screen put him right in the middle of it. He wanted to move his seat back, but it wouldn't budge.

There was Michael Thomas . . . right on the screen in front of Michael Thomas! If he had to give this movie a name, it would be *All the Bad Things That Have Happened to Me in My Life So Far.* There he was—a baby—and it was so real! His mom looked like a teenager, and his father was young and handsome. Mike laughed at the sight of his tough big brother, just a toddler himself, in diapers. Then Mike's grandma was holding him. He missed her so much that it hurt his heart to look at her. She looked so real and alive there that it was hard to believe she was really dead!

The first few movies were actually pretty funny. There he was at three years old—he sure was cute—and playing with his mom's makeup. Lipstick and powder were everywhere, and his mom caught him. Cleaning up the mess was the last thing she needed to do and she was very upset—it was the first time he had been spanked. As Mike sat in his chair in the theater, he suddenly remembered just how he'd felt when it happened. He remembered his hurt bottom and his hurt heart. It felt as if his mom had turned on him. *Gee,* he thought, *you mean I have to feel this stuff all over again, too?* This was starting to feel like some kind of a horror show. Even though he was just a little kid in the film, there were already a few things that had happened that he didn't want to think about. But the memories were coming at him anyway, like a runaway train. *Great.*

Next Mike had to watch his six-year-old self as he was accidentally locked in the bathroom. He remembered how that felt—it wasn't his fault! He hadn't even known how to lock the door in the first place. His dad was really mad that he had to come home from work to take the door off its hinges and free Mike. Mike got a spanking for that, too. His dad didn't even consider that it was an accident. That really hurt. Now he was starting to feel depressed.

Movie after movie played, and now Mike was eight. There he sat on his daily bus ride to school, trying to ignore Henry's mean teasing. Henry was the school bully, who at the time seemed to exist only to make Mike miserable. The other kids wouldn't stick up for Mike because they didn't want any trouble from Henry either.

As the projector clattered on, there was Mike being called over to play basketball with his older brother's friends one day after school. *Oh no.* At first, he'd felt good about it. Those guys actually wanted him to play with them! But they weren't letting him join in their fun—they were making *him* their fun. Instead of trying to make baskets, they all started trying to nail Mike with the basketball. They thought it was very funny, but Mike was crushed. He laughed anyway, pretending that it was pretty funny, but they went off to new adventures, leaving him feeling used and alone.

This stuff hurt. Mike didn't like seeing this at all. What good was this supposed to do anyway? He was starting to get mad that these embarrassing things couldn't just be forgotten forever. He'd already gone through all of this once, wasn't that enough?

More movie reels, and now Mike was ten—"The Cheating Year." Not long after Mike had started the fourth grade, he was accused of cheating even though he hadn't. Another kid had taken some papers with the answers to a quiz from the teacher's desk and put them back in such a messy pile that the teacher could tell someone had moved them. The boy who'd done it accused Mike—he was pretty good at lying and convinced the teacher that Mike had done it. There was the trip to the principal's office, then home for the day. The words kept clanging in his ears: "You're suspended!"

On the way home, riding a special bus, he tried to figure out how in the world he was going to tell his parents about this. How could this have happened to him? Then he relaxed a little bit when he thought, *Surely Mom and Dad will know I didn't do it.* But they didn't. They believed the teacher instead, thinking Mike had cheated to fit in with the other kids. Mike felt so alone, like a stranger in his own home. He knew his parents loved him, but he wished they'd trusted him enough to know he wouldn't cheat—not for any reason. He just wanted to disappear.

Mike had been in the chair for a few hours, but it felt like days—and the movies weren't over yet. He wondered how long he'd have to sit there and watch the movies. He felt as if he were being beaten up! He didn't even feel spiritual anymore. Where did these movies that seemed like memories right out of his head come from? His eyes were glued to the screen when the images were rolling, and he couldn't get the pictures and feelings out of his head when the projector stopped.

A new reel began. It picked up just after Mike had been suspended. Some of the girls in Mike's class thought he was cute, but he overheard them laughing about his clothes. Mike's older brother got all the new clothes, leaving Mike with a bunch of hand-me-downs. By the time Mike fit into the outfits his brother had outgrown, they were no longer cool. Mike tried to ignore the comments, but they really hurt his feelings!

The film played on, but Violet didn't stop to offer Mike any lunch. She knew he wouldn't be hungry after all of this. Each time a reel finished, there was a flapping sound, and the room went dark. Then it was very quiet—only the clicks and clacks of the projector being reloaded broke the tense silence. Mike didn't say a word, and neither did Violet. Then the screen would light up again and continue to show every little detail of Mike's life. Thank goodness it hadn't been too long a life yet! He knew it wouldn't be long now before the films would show the worst day of his life.

Mike knew he could get right up out of that chair if he really wanted to. All of the angels had told him that he had a choice, he was in charge. Right now, he wanted to run. *Please God . . . I don't want to feel that stuff again!* It came anyway, and he just sank lower into his chair.

Mike didn't break down and cry then. He would wait until later that night. He tried to sit up stiffly in his chair and stay as strong as he could. Then it came—the worst day in Mike's life. It was the beginning of the sixth-grade school year. It was a perfect Saturday at the ballpark, and Mike was celebrating with his teammates after a big win. It was such a great day. Mike had hit a home run in the last inning with two runners on base, making the final score 7 to 5. He felt like he was on top of the world. But in the dugout, Bryan made an announcement. He told the team that his dad had to move the family away because of his new job. Mike felt as if he had been hit by a line drive. He remembered the feeling of shock he first felt, followed by the hot tears that welled up in his eyes. He had struggled to keep them back, not wanting to cry in front of everybody.

The film continued, showing Mike over the next few weeks. Most of his time was spent sitting in his dark room. He wasn't hungry for breakfast or for supper. He didn't go to any more games or practices. He kept to himself at school.

Mike sat very still and tried to get away from those memories. He kept feeling as if he was going to cry. This was the hardest thing he'd been asked to do in this angel world so far. Nothing could be worse than having to watch these movies. Mike felt very small. He was exhausted from going through all those emotions again.

There was that flapping sound again, and darkness. Mike could hear Violet loading the projector. More images flooded the screen. There he was, petting Patch. Mike could see the car losing control on the wet street and then hitting him. The movie showed Mike being taken to the hospital, surrounded by frantic doctors and nurses and beeping machines.

The screen went blank, and soon the film began to flap. And it just kept flapping. The lights didn't come on. Mike stood up and tried to see where Violet was in the dark room, but she wasn't there. This was the end of the lesson for the day—the end of the movies. Mike felt really alone.

With the end of the reel still flapping, Mike left the theater and walked down the hallway to his rooms. He wasn't hungry for supper. He was too sad and tired to eat. He fell onto his bed still in his clothes. Violet never came in to say good night.

Mike knew that it was a wise angel who left him alone that night. He didn't feel like talking.

The movies played again and again all night in his dreams. Time after time, he had to see Henry the bully laughing, the principal yelling, and Bryan announcing that he was going to be moving. The memories wouldn't leave him alone, and he finally let go, bawling into his pillow. Seeing Bryan again made him even sadder. It was the second time in this sacred angel land that Mike felt completely abandoned and depressed. He had a lot of reasons to feel that way—and the movies proved it!

* * *

In the morning, Mike's body felt rested, but his mind was dizzy with all that he'd seen in those movies . . . his life had been pretty hard. But he was tough, and even though he didn't understand why he had to see the films, he gritted his teeth and decided not to let them get him down.

After breakfast, Mike went back to his room to get dressed. Beautiful violet clothes had been laid out on his bed by some invisible hands . . . he never saw those helpers who took such good care of him. He put the clothes on and took a deep breath. He felt Violet standing at the door.

The angel didn't make a sound. If Mike had anything to say about having to watch the painful movies, she was giving him a chance to get it off his chest. After a few moments of silence, the angel asked, "Michael Thomas of Pure Intent, is there anything you wish to say or ask?"

"There are more movies, aren't there, Violet?"

"Yes, Michael. More movies."

"Okay . . . let's get it over with." He stood up and waited for her to move.

Violet was surprised. Green was right. This one *was* special—he might actually be one of the few to go all the way Home! He was so young, yet he was more determined and quick to learn than the others she'd taught so far. She thought it was a special honor to be one of Mike's teachers, and she loved him greatly. She turned and led Mike once again to the theater.

He knew what to do. Like a soldier, he took his seat again in the big chair in the front row, dreading the dimming of the lights and the clatter of the projector. But his mind was made up. Nothing would keep him from going Home. *Nothing!*

Again, the movie showed Mike's life, starting from when he was just a toddler. But from the start he could see that this film was different. He would have called it *All the Bad Things I Did in Life.* The mischief that Mike had gotten into as a toddler was funny, and he had a good laugh. It felt good to laugh, but his ribs were still sore from how hard he'd cried the night before.

As Mike got older in the movies, some of the things he'd done began to embarrass him. Surely Violet knew all about these things, but he didn't want to remember them again. As they played out on the screen, he slumped down farther in his chair. He was absolutely uncomfortable and just wanted to hide.

There he was in church at age six, drawing the minister's big ears and big nose on the backs of the little money envelopes. He and his Sunday School buddies stuffed them into the collection basket as it came around. They couldn't wait until after church, when the drawings would be found as the money was counted. They knew the counters would be upset, and they all thought that was pretty funny. Sitting in the violet chair, though, Mike didn't think it was funny at all. He thought that they'd just acted like a bunch of little jerks.

Oh no! Not the car! Now Mike was ten, bored out of his head one Saturday afternoon. He'd snuck out with his mom's car keys to take a little ride in the car. He'd watched his mom closely enough and decided that it was a piece of cake to drive. No problem. The car fired up easily enough and the coast was still clear, so he took a guess as to how to make the car go backwards and jerked on one of the handles beside the steering wheel. It just happened to be the turn signal lever, which immediately broke off in his hand! Afraid he would get caught, he dropped it on the floorboard, turned the car off, and snuck his mom's keys back into her purse.

When Mike's dad got home from work that evening, he noticed the broken turn signal lever as he was putting the car away in the garage for the night. "Mike, have you been playing around with your mom's car? It looks like someone decided to take a little spin and accidentally broke off the turn signal lever."

Mike remembered thinking, *How did he know it was me?* At the time, it had amazed Mike that his dad had figured it out so fast. Now he realized how cool it was that his dad tried to give him a way out by calling it an accident. Sitting in the violet chair watching, Mike felt his skin flush a bright red as he remembered what happened next. He had decided to lie.

"No, sir," the young Mike said, looking straight into his father's eyes.

His dad shrugged. "Must have been one of those little hood-lums at the end of the road." But Mike could tell that his dad knew it was really *him.*

At the time, Mike was ashamed that he'd lied to his dad. He was ashamed now, too. Once again, his dad couldn't trust him, and it made him feel like a stranger. Mike would never forget that.

The repair cost a lot, and some of his mom's household money went to pay for it, so she wasn't able to buy what she'd planned for the week's meals. When he and his parents and his brother sat down for dinner over those next several days, Mike had to see everyone suffer for his bad choice.

Now, Mike was going through it all over again—in living color and 3D. He was really embarrassed that Violet saw what had happened, too. But then Mike realized why his dad didn't believe that he hadn't cheated at school—he had lied about breaking the turn signal just a few weeks before he got suspended. Boy, no wonder his dad couldn't believe him. These movies sure did hurt!

Being accused of something he hadn't done was very hard for Mike to watch. And then seeing himself lie about something he *had* done was even harder. *These movies have to stop!*

Luckily, there was very little, if anything, for Mike to see after that. His whole life had changed when Bryan moved away. He didn't get into any trouble after that. He just did what he was told and spent most of his time in his room. He still missed Bryan so much.

The last movie finally came to an end. This time, the projector was turned off, and the lights came on softly. Violet came up from the back of the room. "Michael, please come with me," she said gently.

Without saying a word, Mike did as she asked. He felt very tired as he got up from the chair he'd been in for so many hours. He hoped that he didn't have to see that chair or that theater ever again.

✳   ✳   ✳

It didn't take long for Mike to figure out that Violet was the kindest angel of all—not *better* than Blue, Orange, or his angel buddy, Green, just different. Each angel had something special that Mike loved. This angel felt soft like his mom and grandma. It was so wonderful to sit across from her and listen to her talk. Everything was fine as long as she was there, just like when he was a little kid with no responsibilities. Now it made sense to Mike that Violet would be the angel in charge of this House of Responsibility. She was like the parent, and Mike was the little boy again.

After the long day in the theater, Violet took Mike into another huge room. It looked to him like the community room at church, but there were only two chairs. There was a display board of some kind on one wall and many symbols and charts on the other walls.

In the other houses, the angels didn't sit much. They never got tired and didn't need to rest. If they sat, it was only to make humans feel more comfortable, just as Violet was doing now as she took the seat across from Mike.

She knew he was still upset about what he'd seen in all the movies and wanted him to get those feelings out. "Michael Thomas of Pure Intent, how do you feel?"

Mike caught on to what Violet was trying to do and said, "You're so wonderful, Violet." He sure felt like crying a lot in this land, and he loved Violet so much right now that it made a big lump in his throat. "I know that you'd never hurt anyone on purpose, but those movies almost did me in! I know I had to see them so that your lessons would sink in somehow before I leave here." He sat quietly for a bit. "How do I feel?" He closed his eyes and thought about how he'd felt over the past few days.

"I feel like a jerk that I did some bad things—I knew they were bad, but I did 'em anyway. It's hard to think I could do that. I thought I was a *good* kid." It had been tough for Mike to watch himself in the movies, but it was even harder to say this out loud to Violet. Mike's mouth was dry. *I could really use a cool drink of water,* Mike thought. Then, out of nowhere, one appeared right in front of him! He took a sip and gave Violet a smile. "Thank you."

Violet could see that Mike was through talking, so she got up and began to speak gently.

"Michael," Violet looked deep into his soul with love so strong that it felt like it came straight from God's heart. "You are a human learning how to go Home, and this is the last time you will feel the hurt of those events." She let Mike sit there and think about this for a minute as she stood up and went over to what looked like a blank wall. She pulled down a rolled-up chart that was mounted at the top of the wall near the ceiling, like the geography maps at school. The chart had some strange writing on it that looked familiar to Mike. *It's the same writing I saw in the map room at the Blue House!* He still couldn't read any of it, though.

"Listen carefully, Michael Thomas of Pure Intent. I am here to explain that you, and all the others in your old life, sat down and carefully planned all that you saw in the movies you've been watching for the last two days."

Mike didn't have a clue what Violet was talking about. "What do you mean, Violet? What I saw were mostly accidents or things that just happened. I didn't plan them."

"You planned all of it with the others, Michael."

"Huh? How?"

"Michael Thomas, you already know that you are a part of God, so you are forever. You are here to learn how to go Home. You want to have the answers to everything, feel peaceful, and have a plan, however you intend it. What you don't remember right now is that you have lived on Earth many times before. You have been many different people and have done all sorts of things. This time, you are Michael Thomas."

Violet continued, "When you are not on Earth, lessons for your next life are planned for you by the only one who knows what you need to learn—*you!* Your teacher at school has to sit down and carefully plan each and every thing she is going to teach you and your classmates. It is the same with you and the others in your group. Some of them agree to be in your life at certain times to cause you problems or to be your enemy. Others agree to show up and help you just in the nick of time. All of these things are planned so that everyone can learn the most and do as much as they can in that life."

This absolutely boggled Mike's mind. "Violet, Bryan was *supposed* to move away from me? He *knew* all along?"

"Not only did you *all* know, Michael, but this was a gift from him to you. To help you to learn that some of the people you love most in your life will not always be with you. They have their own lives to live, other things to do, sometimes somewhere else. You are very young to be learning this, but you will be able to understand soon."

Violet's eyes were so loving. She knew so much about him! She was ready to explain everything, knew how he'd feel about it, and was ready to answer all of his questions. She was awesome.

"It is complicated, Michael," Violet continued. "Each human's life is connected and touches everyone else's. You come in with your lesson plans to learn what you need to learn, to help some people, and to give others problems so they'll learn, too. What looks like an accident is actually planned very carefully."

"That makes it sound like I have no choice—all I'm ever going to do has already been planned for me."

"No, Michael. You can make choices about *all* of your plans. The road is already there, but you can choose to go down it, or go down another one. That is what you are doing now." Violet smiled at Mike, then continued. "When you chose to go Home, you threw away the plans you made with the others. You are way ahead of the plan you made, Michael Thomas! Now you get to see this and understand the big picture."

"But why did I have to watch the movies, Violet?"

"So you could see again what you thought to be bad things in your life, Michael, and understand that you helped make all of that happen so you would be able to learn more. You helped plan all of those situations, and you did them right on schedule. In other words, you were *responsible* for them."

The House of Responsibility. This was a shock, and Mike struggled to understand. "What if I wanted to change it, Violet? Why would I have chosen such troubles and sadness?"

"When you are not in a human body, Michael, you can think clearly, like God can. The body is a heavy vibration, and without it, your vibration is much lighter. You cannot see this now, but it is true. You are *forever,* and all the things that humans do are meant for a bigger purpose than you know—one that you will understand again someday when you take a lighter angelic form like mine. For now, you have to understand that even though troubles and sadness are terrible for you, they are needed for you and Earth to move to a higher vibration, and they are gifts that are very precious! It is the big picture that matters, not each little event. I know this sounds confusing, but it is so."

Violet paused to give Mike a chance to think a bit, then continued.

"And as for changing it? You always have that choice, but most humans don't really know that. It is all part of the test of life, the test of your lessons, Michael. Look at it this way: When you leave here, you will probably stay on the road. The road is the easiest place to be. You don't have to think much about where you are headed. It is already there, leading the way, so why not stay on it? The truth is that in this land of seven houses, the road always goes in the same direction, but it winds around a bit. Therefore, you could probably come to a house sooner if you simply headed in its direction instead of winding around on the road.

You might even discover wonderful new things along the way, off the road. In human life, it is the same." Violet could see that Michael was understanding her just fine, so she continued.

"The road represents the plan you made with the others. It winds around, but it always leads you in the same direction— toward the end of your journey. Most humans stay on the road, never realizing that they can choose to get off it if they wish. It is only when humans leave the road and make their own way that all sorts of things begin to change for them—especially their futures. They actually start writing a *new* future, a *new* plan, as soon as they leave the road. They feel better that they have more control over their own lives, more of a reason to live. Some of them even come through here, Michael." Violet smiled with a twinkle in her eye.

"And this House of Responsibility?" Mike asked.

"It is where you learn that *you*, Michael Thomas of Pure Intent, are the only one responsible for everything that happens in your life. The sadness, the problems, the things that seem to be accidents, all the pain others cause you, and even death. You knew about all of this when you came to this life, you helped plan it with the others, and you played it out—until now."

"But what's the reason for all that?"

"The reason is *love*, Michael. Love at the highest level. The grand plan is something that you will know later. But for now, understand that there is a good reason for it all and you already know this. Things are not always as they seem."

The words rang in Mike's ears. *Things are not always as they seem . . .* those were the words of the first angel, the one in the vision after his accident. Then he'd heard it again from the other angels along the way. Mike's mind was like a tornado, whirling around, trying to understand all this new information. It was hard. Then he remembered Blue's words in the House of Maps. *You are looking at the contracts of every human being on the planet.* In those small holes that Blue guarded, millions of them, were the life plans of all humans . . . carefully planned and ready to go, yet also ready to be changed if humans made the choice.

The true meaning of all this suddenly hit Mike like a hammer. "Violet, why didn't I hear about this before? Why doesn't anyone talk about this on Earth, like in church?"

"You hear a lot about God in church, Michael, but not everything. Sometimes you only get to hear about what some humans *think* about God."

Mike was relieved that Violet didn't put his church down. He'd had some good times there. "But was my minister wrong in not telling us, Violet?"

"Michael, the truth is always the truth from wherever you receive it, and there are bits and pieces of it in *all* of your churches. Humans are greatly honored for trying to learn more about God and how to be more like Him. Your churches tell you about love, miracles, and a little about how things really work. That is why you felt the Spirit of God when you went there, Michael. When humans search for God, Spirit honors that search, even when the human doesn't know much about Him. The honor is in the searching, not in what you got right. So, the holiness of your planet is in the humans who walk on it, not in all the beautiful churches."

Violet moved over to the chart she'd pulled down earlier. "You know how holy your Bible is, right? Well, take a look at this." She pointed to the strange writing on the chart. "This is what is called the *Akashic Record* of humans. It has all the records of your lives and your possible plans or contracts." She paused with deep respect. "Michael, this is the most sacred writing in the Universe, and it was written and worked out by those who chose to be humans!"

Violet looked right at Mike, and he understood her meaning. He realized that she was acting this way to show her respect for *him*—spiritual respect! This made him feel bashful and uncomfortable, but he wanted to know more.

The next few days in the House of Responsibility were awesome. Mike came to understand what it really meant to be alive as a human. He learned more about who he was, and who he had *been*. It all came together like one giant puzzle. Violet showed him the records and contracts he'd made with some of the people in his life so far. Mike didn't get to see anything that was actually planned for later in his life, but he was beginning to get a better idea of how all this worked.

The most amazing information Mike learned was that humans are actually pieces of God, but they walk the earth without knowing this so that they can learn their lessons better. The better they learn, the more they change the earth itself! Violet kept saying that humans were the honored ones. This was a new twist . . . Mike was used to thinking that angels were the only honored ones.

✳ ✳ ✳

Finally, it was time to go. Mike felt that everything he'd learned from Violet made him much more powerful. As he put on his battle gear to begin his journey to the next house, he could hear Orange's words: *The Sword of Truth . . . the Shield of Knowledge . . . the Armor of Wisdom.* Things were beginning to make a lot more sense. He recognized now that the weapons were ceremonial symbols of his purpose. Many of the words he had heard on his journey were being repeated, explained, and finally understood.

Violet led Mike to the front door of the house. "Michael Thomas of Pure Intent, I'll miss you."

"I feel like I'm *leaving* Home, not *going* Home!" Mike was well taken care of in The House of Responsibility, and Violet felt like family. So far he'd met four wonderful angels. *What's next?*

"More family, Michael," Violet answered his thoughts.

At the door, Mike saw that his shoes were right where he'd left them, and he remembered being asked why he thought he was supposed to leave them there. He looked at the shoes and then back at Violet. "There's one thing more, Violet."

"Yes, Michael. I remember. Now *you* can tell me why," she smiled at him and waited patiently for the answer.

Mike knew, but he was too embarrassed to say it. It seemed like bragging to him.

"Say it, Michael." Violet was the teacher again.

"Because the human is sacred." There . . . he said it. "And because this house is where humans walk in a high vibration."

Violet sighed, and Mike could see that she was proud of him. "I could not have wished for a finer answer, Michael Thomas of Pure Intent," she said. "It is the human, and not the angel, who makes this place sacred. Michael, you are indeed a special human being. I honor God within you! Now, I have a question for you."

Mike knew the question but let her ask him anyway.

"Michael, do you love God?"

"Yes, Violet, I do." Tears were coming to his eyes, and he wasn't afraid to let her see this. He was sorry to leave this beautiful place, where he'd met with wonderful soft energy. He turned and walked a few steps, then turned around again. "I'll miss you, too, Violet, but you'll be here in my heart."

He started down the path to the next house, then turned back to say one more thing to the watching angel. "Hey, Violet, watch me!"

Michael Thomas left the path and started out over the green, sweet-smelling grass. He looked back and shouted at her. "Look at me! I've decided to make my own path!" He laughed at his little joke, and skipped and hopped in the grass until the Violet House was out of sight.

Violet stood and watched Mike until he disappeared over the next hill. Like a mother, she was proud indeed of this great being called Michael Thomas. Then she went back inside and closed the door. She went back to her regular form, which was not like a human, but it was glorious. Then Violet said: "If this is what the new breed of human is like, we are in for a wild spiritual ride indeed!"

* * *

A bit farther up the road, a sickening IT had found a place to hide and wait. The trap IT had prepared was perfect . . . the adventure was all over for that puny Michael Thomas. *While he's looking back over his shoulder for me, I'll attack him from the front. He won't know what hit him!* The disgusting creature chuckled at how clever it was becoming in this fairyland. *It won't be long now . . .*

IT knew that the little human was out of the house now and traveling again. IT could feel it!

IT would have a long wait, though. Michael Thomas had left the road.

* * * * * *

Chapter Nine
The Fifth House

It didn't take Mike long to realize that the journey was a bit tougher off the path. He had to keep checking the position of the sun to make sure he was still traveling in the right direction. He also had to keep looking at his map so he wouldn't accidentally pass up the next house. The open fields were much more difficult to walk through than the smooth road had been, and Mike was afraid that this wouldn't be much of a shortcut.

Even with all of these challenges, Mike realized that at least this time the journey was more fun. He was also trying to prove to himself that he could make a change anytime, anywhere—even in a spiritual land.

This one off-road adventure was enough, though. Mike decided he'd follow the path again when he left the next house— it was easier. It felt good to know that he had choices, and Mike didn't feel like he could only travel one way or the other.

Mike soon realized that he was no longer being followed. *Has the spell been broken? Has the creepy stalker gone away? Probably not.* Mike figured that he must have fooled the evil thing by leaving the road, but IT would figure out Mike's trick soon enough. Mike stayed ready for any surprise attack.

About four hours later, as Mike was walking over some flat grassland, the sky started getting dark. He knew what that meant! Another one of those weird, terrifying storms was about to strike. *I'd better look around for shelter immediately.* Mike remembered that in the last storm, a screeching wind had him flat on the ground in ten minutes, praying for his very life.

Mike took out the map again. Sure enough, the trusty map was still current, and the red dot showed what was around him. It showed a nearby rock outcropping that had a cave-like shelter in it. He rolled up the map and stuffed it back in its pouch, then walked toward the rocks.

Even though it took Mike only a few minutes to get to the rocks, the storm was already getting worse. The sky was much blacker and the winds were starting to howl. Mike saw the cave's opening and hurried to it. As soon as he stepped inside, the rain started blowing and the wind let loose. He scrambled to the back of the cave for shelter. It was totally amazing to him how wild the weather could get here. He whispered a thank you to Blue for the map that saved him at the very last minute, taking him out of harm's way once again.

Mike crouched in the cave, watching the storm rage and wail.

"When the human is not here, there are no storms." Mike looked around, startled by the voice that echoed through the cave. It was Blue's voice, but Blue was not there!

"Blue? Is that you?" Mike called out to the dark corners of the cave.

"Yes, Michael Thomas." Mike could hear Blue laugh. *"You've learned to use the map! Believe it or not, there have been humans like you on this journey who threw the map away, thinking it must be no good. You have learned how it is to be in the* Now—*you see the storm coming, you look at your map, and you can get out of the storm before it gets bad. Michael, you are dearly loved!"*

Mike smiled. It was all for HIM! All this energy—all this planning! He looked outside and yelled at the wind, "You can stop now. I'm safe!"

The storm lasted about two hours, until the sun began to set. Mike didn't know if he could reach the next house before dark, and without the sun, he didn't know if he could even find it. But he felt safe anyway and knew he could defend himself if he had to. He left the cave, watched where the sun was going down, and headed out again in the direction he figured was north.

Mike made only slow progress in the dark. He suddenly realized that he'd never been out at night in this land before. *Would there be stars or a moon?* He quickly found out—there was nothing but pitch black sky. When the last rays of sunlight faded, it was absolutely dark. With no light at all, he couldn't even see his map. *I should have stayed in the cave.* He wasn't ready for this kind of blackness! He couldn't see where he was going at all anymore, and he didn't want to get lost, so he sat down in the damp grass to wait.

After about an hour of sitting in the dark, Mike noticed something strange off in the distance. He had been walking toward a distant hill earlier in the day. But since the sun had set and it had gotten dark, he had lost sight of his destination—until now. A strange red glow like the setting sun gradually grew brighter. It was coming from behind the hill. Something over there was giving off light!

Mike stood up slowly and began to inch forward very carefully. The faint glow allowed him to see the ground right around his feet. He moved on, cautiously and quietly pushing his feet forward through the grass, toward the glowing red light. Stooped over, eyes straining to see, he moved ahead a little bit at a time.

Mike struggled forward like this for a while. And when he finally reached smooth ground, he almost stumbled! The road! Even though he'd decided earlier not to take it, the road found him when he needed it the most. What a place!

Even though the road didn't lead straight to the hill Mike had been traveling toward, he believed it would lead him to the next house—it was heading in the direction of the red glowing light.

The closer Mike got to the glowing light, the better he could see. Still, he was careful. He didn't know what the light *was,* and he wanted to be ready for anything.

Mike came around the next curve and couldn't believe what he saw. The glow! There in the forest was the next house glowing bright red! While the other houses had given off a soft glow from inside, this one was as bright as a red moon! Then Mike saw the sign: House of Relationships. That stopped him in his tracks. *Relationships? I don't know anything about that stuff. They'll probably just show me more films.*

"Yes, we will!" A young red angel appeared out of nowhere on the steps leading to the door. "Greetings, Michael Thomas of Pure Intent. I thought we'd lost you!"

"No way! I just had to take my time. I guess I wasn't in a hurry to see any more films. Yours aren't like Violet's, are they?"

"No, Michael, they're not." The red angel was as handsome as a movie star, like an action hero with huge muscles. He was really big! There was a holy look about the angel's red robes, but he put Mike instantly at ease because he was very friendly and talkative.

"Are you hungry, Michael Thomas?"

"Yes, sir!"

Red led Mike into the house. Just as Violet had done before, Red asked Mike to take his shoes off as he entered the house.

As with the other houses, the outside of this house didn't seem any bigger than a small cottage. But on the inside, it was HUGE. There were stairs and arches, and windows that looked out on exotic landscapes. Mike hadn't noticed anything but grass and rocks on his walk, but looking out these windows, he saw that they were surrounded by lush gardens and waterfalls. It was all very strange—it reminded Mike of *Alice in Wonderland.* He smiled at the thought. *Guess I should start looking for the white rabbit!*

"White is next, Michael," Red said. "No rabbit, though."

Mike laughed. *So the next house is white? Hmm . . . the White House. That's funny . . . the President lives in the White House!* Red also thought that was funny, and Mike had a good feeling about the lessons he'd learn here. He no longer felt like a stranger in this land of angels.

"Are we feeling like family, Michael?" Red stopped at the dining room. Mike could smell the dinner that was already waiting on the table.

"Yes, Red." Mike was finally starting to get used to the angels knowing his thoughts.

"Well, you are correct. That is what this house is all about." He turned and took Mike into the dining room. As usual, an amazing meal was waiting.

"I'll see you in the morning, Michael Thomas. Sleep well and be at peace with your lesson here." Red turned to leave. "Good night," said the angel as he shut the door.

Mike laughed at how well mannered the angels had become. He did indeed feel peaceful. Mike was sure that Red knew all about his lessons in the Violet House and what he went through learning them. He thought it was kind of Red to let him know that the next lessons were going to be different.

Mike sat down at the large banquet table full of delicious food. He ate like a horse! The storm had caused him to miss lunch, and the difficult travel in the darkness had really tired him out—more than he realized. After dinner, he immediately fell asleep. He was peaceful and comfortable and safe in this fine red house. His sleep was deep and calm—almost as if he were already Home.

* * *

Late that night, while Michael Thomas was sleeping in his soft red bed, an angry, foul beast crept up the road toward the Red House. IT took one look at the house and knew that Michael Thomas was in it. IT had waited and waited on the road outside the Violet House, but Michael Thomas never came.

IT raged inside, burning with an anger that made it very determined. But it was confused! How had Michael Thomas known it was there waiting? He must have gone a different way, not following the road at all! He actually made it to the Red House without the road! *How?*

IT knew the angels weren't allowed to butt in, and they couldn't tell Michael about IT. But IT would have to come up with new plans. When it had gone ahead of Michael, it had lost him. The nasty creature decided to follow Mike again. That way, at least, IT would know where Mike was.

As before, IT found a place in the trees to watch and wait for Mike to leave the Red House. IT passed the time by thinking about destroying the pesky kid once and for all. Over and over, IT made plans about how to catch Mike and what to do with him. IT would have to be very strong and use some tricks, but IT knew what was important to Michael Thomas and how he thought. IT began plotting. IT would hide and wait again. *Trickery is the key.*

* * *

As usual, clothes were already waiting for Mike in the closet when he got up. They were fresh and clean—and red.

Mike enjoyed the delicious breakfast that was waiting for him in the next room. He'd just finished taking his last bites when Red knocked on the door and came in.

"I see that you are well rested and ready to go, Michael."

"That I am, Red." Mike was very polite and feeling good. "Thank you for the wonderful food."

"You deserve all of it, Michael Thomas of Pure Intent." Red smiled and motioned for Mike to get up and walk with him. He led Mike to places in the House of Relationships that they hadn't gone through the night before. This house was different from the others. All the red made Mike feel awake and full of energy.

They went into a large theater. There was the same wrap-around screen as at Violet's, and the same big padded chair, except that it was red. This chair was much closer to the screen than the chair at Violet's had been. *Uh-oh,* Mike thought, remembering how real the movies had seemed before. *Don't tell me I'm going to be even closer to the action!*

"It is not what you think, Michael Thomas."

"Thank you, my friend," Mike said, a little relieved. "Should I sit down now?"

"Please do."

Red went to the back of the room and started the projector. Mike sat in his seat of honor in front, and the show began.

The movie played, but there was no sound. Instead, Red talked and explained what Mike was seeing. It was more like a slide show than a movie.

"This is all about your family, Michael," Red began, as the screen lit up with pictures. "You already learned in the Violet House that you and your loved ones have been on your planet many times as many people. You also learned that before each life begins, you have the chance to make many careful plans with those people. It is time you understood more. Let me start by introducing your family to you again."

Red showed Mike 27 beautiful faces on the screen. Their names were long and strange. Red recited the names aloud: Angenon, Aleelu, Borifee, Vereeifon, Kuigre, and on and on. Next, Red showed Mike a chart of his family tree, so he could see those who came before him and how they all fit into the big plan. But this was like no family tree Mike had ever seen. At the top of the chart were people Mike expected: his parents and grandparents, and his brother. But also on the chart were his friends from church and school, teachers, his old baseball coach, and Mrs. Burns. Bryan, too! Then came some strangers. He took a minute to try to remember each one. There were lines connecting all of them. So many lines! This was hard.

While Mike studied the chart, Red explained that each line was a lifetime. These people had been with him many times, with many names and many roles to play so that all their lessons could be learned.

"Now it is time to hear their stories, Michael." Mike wasn't ready for what happened next in that red theater with the wonderful red angel.

The first picture on the chart suddenly zoomed to full size on the screen and started moving! There was sound, too. It was Bryan! Alive on the screen! Then Bryan stepped off the screen, onto the floor right in front of Mike. He was real—no longer part of any movie or slide show! He called Mike by name and began his story.

"Michael Thomas, I am Reeneuy from Quadril Five. I am your family, and I love you dearly! You knew me as your best friend, Bryan, in this life. Before that, I was your brother, David. Before I was David, I was your wife, Cynthia. Michael Thomas of Pure Intent, we have a contract, a plan, and the energy of it is called *karma*. We planned together to meet again in this life, and so we did. I was to help you learn about close friends, and how the people you love the most have to go away sometimes to make way for the *other* things in your plan—and the other things in *their* plans. You and your loved ones may not always be together. You and I finished something we both started hundreds of years ago, and we did it well. It's my gift to you, and yours to me. We did it together!"

Mike's mouth fell open. Bryan—or Reeneuy from Quadril Five—wasn't just some picture on the screen. He was real! His very best friend was telling him that yes, he'd been his buddy this time—but before that he was someone else he knew . . . and before that . . . it went on and on. This was all shown to Mike with so much patience and love! He could feel the truth of it. *But how weird!*

"Thank you, Bryan. Dear friend!" Mike bowed in appreciation. Now he was able to see everything in a different light. He used to think that Bryan had ruined everything by moving away. But now Mike realized that Bryan was just trying to help him learn. And he knew that they would meet again. Bryan smiled back and slowly disappeared.

The next picture came forward and told another complicated story of love and tough situations. It was Mr. Burroughs, Mike's fifth-grade teacher. Mr. Burroughs explained that he'd also been with Mike many times, as many people. This time he was supposed to help Mike with his schooling, and he'd done his job. He explained how Mike had also helped *him*. Mike couldn't figure out how he might have helped a teacher until Mr. Burroughs explained that Mike was a good, courteous student, and helped the afternoons go by easier. Mike thanked him, and Mr. Burroughs's picture faded.

Other people came down from the screen to tell their wonderful and amazing stories. They also told Mike how much they loved him. Mike thanked each and every one. It was unbelievable! He was so happy that he could see these people and hear their stories. How could he be sad about Bryan's not being with him anymore, now that he understood that they were together before and would be together again?

There was time for only nine stories that day, and then the lights came on. Mike sat quietly, realizing that the day had gone by and he hadn't even needed a break for lunch. Red came up to the front of the room and stood before Mike.

"Tired?"

"No—this is exciting! Do we have to stop?"

Red laughed and motioned for Mike to stand.

"There will be two more days of this, Michael Thomas, with time enough for most of the family to speak." Mike had about a million questions as he followed Red to the dining room.

"Will you stay for dinner, Red? I mean, I know you don't eat, but I'd like to ask you some questions if you don't mind."

Red smiled. "I'd be happy to stay, Michael."

They went into the dining room. It surprised Mike to see that two places were set.

"Who's joining us?"

"I thought you invited me," joked Red.

"But you don't eat!"

"Says who?" Red was having fun, as he sat across the table from Mike and poured himself a tall glass of juice. Mike was still confused.

"I never—I mean—none of the other angels ate. I just thought—"

Red interrupted Mike. "Michael, angels don't have to eat, but I'm going to sit here and eat with you because humans like to have someone to eat and talk with them. Right?"

"Right." Mike had to agree. It had been weeks since he'd been able to sit down and enjoy a meal with anyone. Green had sat and kept him company, but not one of the angels ever shared in the food. They sat down to enjoy the dinner that had been laid out for them. Although everything was delicious, Mike's thoughts quickly turned back to his experience in the theater.

"Red, what just happened . . . was that real? I mean, when they were speaking to me—was that just some kind of angel way of doing movies?"

Red laughed again, wiping his chin with a napkin. "Why is it that humans will believe in something only if can happen in *their* world? If it cannot, then they think it's a trick. I'll never understand that."

"Well?" Mike persisted.

"It was absolutely real. More real than your Earth world, Michael. To be here for you in person, your family had to come to this house."

Mike didn't completely understand but kept the questions coming anyway.

"Red, all their names were so strange—do I have a name like that?"

"Your name is hidden for now, Michael. You will know it in time, at least the part of it you can speak—but it is not important to your lessons here. After all, you don't know my name, and it has not stopped you from enjoying yourself." Red took another bite.

Mike had never really thought that the angels might have other names. He just automatically called them by their colors. It was easy, and they had told him it was okay. "Red, what's your real name?" Mike was really interested.

"You think that a name is just a sound, Michael."

Mike noticed that Red really didn't do a very good job of eating. You could tell that it was his first time. The food kept falling out of his mouth back onto the plate. He'd already gone through four napkins and was trying his best to hold his fork just like Mike. It was really funny, but Mike was so interested in his questions that he didn't say anything about it. Later he would have a good laugh. But right now, he wanted to learn.

Red continued, wiping his mouth again. "The names of all beings in the Universe are energy, including yours and mine. They have color, vibration, sound—even intent! They cannot be given as a sound in the air as your Earth name can. Even the names you saw and heard today are only part of the energy of those humans' real names. When spiritual beings greet each other, they can 'see' each other's names, their whole story shown by the colors and vibrations of their angelic body—called a *Merkabah*. It is very complicated . . . more than you can understand right now, Michael."

"Red, today when you showed me the pictures of my family, only some of them stepped off the screen to talk to me. There were a lot of others who got skipped over. Why?" Mike was really curious about the beautiful red-haired woman who was in the top row. She was the most beautiful woman he'd ever seen. He just had to know how she figured into all this.

"Those are humans you have not met in your life on Earth yet, Michael. The unfulfilled contracts." Red took a big gulp of

his juice, and some dribbled down the sides of his mouth. There went napkin number seven.

Mike sat back for a minute and thought about what Red had said. *Unfulfilled contracts?* His decision to go Home was starting to feel wrong. He probably would have met that beautiful red-haired woman when he got older . . . *That could have been my WIFE I was looking at!* And all those other people: He'd made plans with all of them. *What have I messed up by deciding to go Home?*

Red was listening and answered his unspoken question. "Michael, listen to me. Not everything you are thinking about can be completely understood. Your mind doesn't work like God's yet, and you cannot know all that we know at this point in your journey. You are still human and are greatly loved for being just that. There is more happening here than you know. You chose to leave the road, and your choice is honored—there is no right or wrong to it. We would not be helping you on your holy quest if it was not meant to be."

Mike had never thought of his choice to go Home as a holy quest. It had just been a way of getting out of a life he wasn't happy in. He was in training to go Home, and for some reason was honored and blessed by these angels. Red was right. He didn't see the big picture. "Will I ever understand?"

"When you stand before the door to go Home and open it, you will understand." Red stood up and graciously excused himself.

Mike got up and walked around the table to the chair where Red had sat eating with him. It looked like a three-year-old had eaten there! Crumbs, juice, and pieces of food were everywhere. Mike burst out laughing. "I gotta love ya, Red!" He realized how thoughtful it was for Red to sit down and eat with him. He'd tried. *I guess angels have things they can't do, too.* Then he thought more deeply and wondered, *If there are things angels can't do, and*

angels are part of the big picture, I wonder if there are things God can't do? Mike heard an answer immediately. It was Violet!

"Yes, God can't lie. God can't hate. God can't help some people more than others. This is why you have to learn so many lessons on Earth, so everyone has the same chance to learn and grow."

Mike listened carefully, but still he did not understand everything the angel said. *Maybe in time this will make sense to me.* It was good to hear Violet's voice again.

Mike slept, but the two angel names Annyehoo and Ellyuin kept appearing to him, with wonderful colors and geometric patterns. The colors and lights danced in his head, but Mike still managed to sleep peacefully and soundly.

* * *

The next day, Mike could hardly wait to get started. He wolfed down his breakfast and followed Red to the theater. He actually ran to the big padded chair and waited for more stories from his family. He was surprised to see that the first person to come down from the screen today was Henry the bully.

Henry was just as big and mean-looking as Mike remembered. Henry told Mike how hard their plans were to make. He and Mike had been sailors on a ship together in another life, and the way that life went forced them to learn certain lessons in this one. Mike thought this was much more interesting than social studies back at school. As Henry faded, Mike thanked him for playing his part so well. It felt weird to be able to thank Henry for something!

Bryan's father spoke next, enjoying the chance to explain his role to Mike. He was a guy who made things happen. He was proud that he'd brought Mike his biggest lesson yet. He'd made an appointment in Mike's life to move his family away. He knew this would leave Mike without a best buddy, but he'd done it

anyway—right when he was supposed to. Bryan's dad talked about the planning meeting, and how all the family had clapped their hands when the meeting was over. They were all so happy about the plans they'd made. Leaving people behind just wasn't the same for those on the other side. Bryan's dad wasn't sorry for taking Bryan away—and he didn't have to be now because Mike understood why it had to happen.

Mike said, "Thank you for your great gift," and he meant it.

Nine more members of his family told Mike their stories that day. Then, the session was over, so Mike got up and went to dinner. This time Mike didn't ask Red to eat; he was just happy to have company. Angels were good at a lot of things, but eating wasn't one of them!

After he'd finished chewing a big bite of freshly baked bread, Mike paused. "Red, those people I've been talking to from my life are still living on Earth. So how can they be here to tell me their stories?"

"Again, Michael Thomas, don't think of the way things happen in your world. The real Michael Thomas can be many places. You don't have to stay in just one place. You only need a part of the piece of God that is your soul to be in your body as you live on Earth. The higher part of you can be doing other things in other places, like working on new plans if changes need to be made." Red smiled while Mike tried to absorb what had just been said.

"New plans, Red?"

"Yes, Michael."

It was all starting to fit together. There were planning meetings before Mike began his life on Earth, and there were also planning meetings throughout his life once it had started. He could be on Earth and at these meetings, using a part of him he didn't even know about!

"It makes me sound like I'm split into pieces, Red."

"Michael, close your eyes." Red was giving Mike another lesson. "Think. Remember what you saw and heard today. Imagine yourself back in the theater, in your big red chair." Mike did so.

Red continued, "Now, where are you?"

"In the theater, in my big red chair."

"I thought you were here eating."

Mike opened his eyes and looked at Red. "Wait a minute, that's only my imagination. It doesn't count any more than my dreams do. My real body is here. My thoughts are in the theater."

"Okay, Michael, which is real—your body or your thoughts?" Red asked.

"My body . . . I think." Red didn't give a direct answer. Instead, he leaned forward and gave Mike something else to think about. "Michael, last night . . . you met with Bryan again, you know. This time you saw his real energy, and you called him by his real name. You traveled places with him and had a great time."

Mike stopped eating.

"It is true." Red assured him.

"But I was asleep—dreaming!"

"Your human-ness still prevents you from understanding how Spirit really works. Now this is going to be hard to understand, but please try. Wherever your thoughts are, *you* are. Here's an example. The teacher is at the front of the class, explaining the assignment. You are trying to pay attention, but your thoughts drift away—perhaps you are daydreaming about the time you went to the carnival and rode the scariest ride. Your teacher notices that you are not paying attention. She calls your name and asks, 'Where in the world *are* you?' You see, you were not really there in the classroom. Your body was right there at your desk, but your consciousness was at the carnival again, and your consciousness is what is real. The body lasts only a short time. It is holy, but it is still only the container that holds the spirit of your consciousness—the real you—and you can take that spirit anywhere you want. So, you see, wherever your thoughts are, *you* are. Believe me, it is so." Red smiled.

"I can leave my body?" Mike was puzzled.

"You can do it all the time, Michael!" Red chuckled. "This puts you in two places at the same time. It is not as strange as you might think!

"Is there a part of me that's not here?" Mike asked.

"Yes." Red knew what the next question would be.

"Where is it?"

Red got up from his seat and headed toward the door so Mike could get ready for bed. He turned to honor the last question. "It is in the most holy of places, with all the others. It is in the Temple of Physics. It is with God." Red left.

Mike was hearing all kinds of new information and couldn't understand any of it. *The Temple of Physics? What is that? It sounds like a church science project, or like something from* Star Wars. *What could Red mean?* It seemed like every answer Red gave just made Mike ask more questions.

Mike went to bed, but just before he fell asleep, he remembered what Red had said about his dreams being real. Had he really traveled somewhere last night with Bryan? If he did, why didn't he remember more about it? Mike was still thinking about this as he drifted off to sleep. In his dreams, he traveled to be with some of the family who'd told him their stories over the last two days. They laughed and talked with love about their plans together. But he wouldn't remember any of it when he woke up.

* * *

It was the last day in the Red House. In the theater, a few more family members told their stories. Mike honored the fact that they were family and had done so much together so far. Now Mike knew more than most humans did about his spiritual family and plans for life. He wished he'd known all of this before—things might have been a lot different. It wouldn't have hurt him so much to lose Bryan. He'd have gotten back on the baseball team or just made new friends. It wouldn't have bothered him as much when Henry the bully picked on him. Any problems he encountered would be small potatoes—Mike would know that he'd planned them himself so he could learn more. In a way, Mike was sad that he wouldn't be going back to his old life with this new understanding.

That night, Mike felt his body hinting at another change in vibration. He got ready for it exactly as he had been taught in the green House of Biology. He remembered that as the Spirit raises its vibration, the body must also change so it can better hold increased energy. Mike knew that Spirit was carried in each cell of his body. A few hours later, Mike felt that his body had made the change, and that it was time to leave the Red House. No sooner had he laid his head on the pillow than he was fast asleep.

After another delicious breakfast, he put on all of his battle gear and went to meet Red, who was already standing at the front door of the house. As Mike walked up, Red said, "Michael Thomas of Pure Intent, you have changed."

"I know." Mike was bashful about it. "How can you tell, Red? How can an angel tell if a human has changed to a higher vibration?"

Red was still looking at Mike proudly. "Your colors give you away. Never has a human changed so much so quickly, Michael.

You made the most of what we taught you. You are indeed a special human!"

Mike walked into the sunlight and found his shoes right where he'd left them. He hadn't understood what Red meant by his colors, but it didn't matter. "I shall never forget this place, my Red Friend. Here I met my family for the first time."

Red smiled. He knew the truth. Mike had met his real family for the first time as Michael Thomas, the human. "Michael Thomas, you are still in for many surprises in the two houses to come. Your new vibration will make these all the more intense. Are you ready?"

Mike didn't know if he liked the sound of that. "Is there a problem ahead, Red?" he asked nervously.

"Expect some challenges before you get to the door marked Home," Red answered, a serious look in his eyes. "These may be the greatest challenges you have faced here so far. Some may try to discourage you from going Home. They may try to fool you into believing that all of this isn't real. Some may even scare you."

Mike straightened up when he heard this, knowing that some kind of terrible test must be awaiting him. But he was determined. He had come this far—he wouldn't back down. "I understand. I'm ready."

"Indeed you are, my little human friend. I have a question. You'll hear it this morning, and only two more times. The last time will be the most important one."

Finally! Mike was glad that the angel was giving more information about why this same question was asked at every house. *It must have to do with the seventh house and what I'll find there.* "I'm ready for the question, Red." He knew the question but wanted to give Red the honor of asking it.

Red could tell that Mike was letting him have his moment, and he appreciated it. "Michael Thomas of Pure Intent, do you love God?"

"As I do you, and all the others—yes, I love God." Mike stepped forward and did something he hadn't done before. He hugged Red! The large red angel was tough to get his arms around, but he did his best.

Red quickly accepted the physical good-bye and stooped down to let Mike hug him at eye level. He surrounded Mike completely, swallowing him up in his flowing red robes.

"There's great meaning to this, Michael," Red said as he let go of Mike. "You are the first human to visit here who has had a vibration strong enough to touch an angel." Red was choked up. "We've never been able to hug humans in the past. I'll always remember this."

Mike proudly accepted the compliment and then walked down to the road knowing he had a choice—to take the road or to make his own way. He chose to follow the road to the next house, which he already knew was white. He turned one more time and waved to Red.

* * *

In no time, the sneaking, stinky creature jumped down out of the tree it had been hiding in and began to follow the little human. IT left no footprints as it moved along the edges of the path. IT passed very close to Red and gave him an ugly look with eyes of fire.

For the first time, Red spoke to IT. "Spook, you haven't got a chance." With that, Red turned around and disappeared into the glowing house of his color.

* * * * * *

Chapter Ten

The Sixth House

The walk to the sixth house was easy enough, but Mike could feel that IT was back. But Mike wasn't afraid . . . he just paid closer attention. He noticed that he could actually feel the creature's dark energy following not too far behind. He absolutely felt that this energy was real!

On the journey to the last house, Mike had sensed danger on the road. He hadn't been able to feel the creature's energy before. But now, it was as if Mike had been given the gift of super feeling. What did all of this mean? What or who was this—thing? What did IT want? Why didn't IT quit hiding? Why was IT following him all the time?

Mike thought back about the storm. The dark greenish figure had come out and attacked him while the storm was at its worst—IT disappeared only when that lightning struck. *Maybe IT's afraid of me,* Mike thought.

But his intuition told him that soon he'd have to meet the thing on the road for a fight to the finish. Red had even hinted at it. And he kept hearing, *"Be careful, Mike!"* in his head—the angels were giving him advice.

As Mike went on, he saw the thing twice out of the corner of his eye as he looked back. At least IT was behind him. Mike thought that if IT were smart, it would get ahead of him on the road between the sixth and seventh houses. *Better watch out for that,* he mused.

Mike took out his map to see if any of the shadowy creature's energy would show up around the red dot. The map showed all the things around him for a good distance, but no trace of his evil stalker. Mike looked back to where he'd last seen something move, then realized that the thing managed to stay far enough away not to show up on the map. *Could IT possibly know how my map works?*

The White House appeared not long after noon. It looked small like the other houses. Mike walked up to it and looked for its sign. He knew that the sign would give him a hint about what kind of lessons he'd learn there. There was a sign, all right . . . it read *House of Love.* This was curious. Certainly all the other angels loved him very much—and he'd already been through the House of Relationships. Yet here was a whole house set aside for love.

Mike turned off the road and walked up to the door. No one came to greet him. He looked for the usual place to put his shoes, and it was there, waiting for him. He wondered if he should wait for a white angel, but decided not to. He put his shoes in their place, opened the door, and went inside.

The smell of flowers floated all around him. He remembered that smell! He walked down the hallway to a huge white area. Then he remembered . . . this was where he had been after the accident! Suddenly, the great white angel who'd been with him then stood before him.

"Greetings, Michael Thomas of Pure Intent! We meet again," the angel said with a brilliant smile!

Mike was very pleased to see this wonderful angel again. The way his robes flowed around him amazed Mike all over again. The angel seemed to blend right into the house. And he floated up above the ground! He seemed much more holy than the other angels, too, if that was possible. The other angels had become Mike's friends, his family—but this one reminded Mike of a minister. Mike sensed that there was a great energy within this angel.

Mike smiled up at White. "You have a face this time." The angel's face had been blurry the first time Mike saw him.

"Indeed, I do, and it is because you have made it this far that you are able to see it. You have done very well, Michael. Your vibration is higher than that of any human who has traveled here. Already there are colors in your name that tell me this—colors that will be there forever no matter what happens, whether you go on to the next house or not."

There was that warning again! *Do they think I'm not going to make it?* Red had given him the same feeling—that maybe something bad might happen close to the end of his sacred journey. *What's coming that could be so tough?*

"This house will make you think twice about going on," said White, again reading Mike's thoughts. "Not everything is as it seems. Always remember this, and you will do well as you deal with what is to come."

Mike remembered that he was standing in front of the angel who'd first said those words to him, and how true they'd been! It reminded him that he needed to think everything through very carefully.

"This is the House of Love. It is next to the purest house you will ever go into. It is not a house of lessons as the others were; it is the main house. The center."

"But it's number six out of seven—in a row of houses!"

"Again, not everything is as it seems." The angel smiled. "Believe me, it is the center. The order of the houses exists only for your lesson, Michael, and was arranged so that you may understand things here better."

Mike had to know more about the house. "What will I find here?"

"Answers . . . "

The angel floated closer to Mike. What a face he had! If love had a face, then this was it: Beautiful, wonderful, and peaceful. Mike just wanted to close his eyes and stand by White for a while and rest.

White went on with his answers. "This is a journey into making choices. A study again of all that is. Another step up in your vibration, if you want it."

"Who are you, really, White? You're not just the white angel in the sixth house. I know that much."

"I AM known by all, Michael Thomas—and THAT I AM known by all; therefore, I exist."

This was the very same answer White had given him the first time he'd asked, right after the accident. It still made no sense to him.

"I don't understand your answer at all, White, but I know I will someday. Of all the angels I've met so far, you're by far the grandest." Mike was telling the truth. He understood that the angel in front of him was one of great importance and power.

"That may be so, Michael Thomas, but there is one coming who is grander than us all." White waited for Mike to think this over, then turned and floated ahead, leading him through blurry hallways that led here and there. Mike couldn't see clear outlines of rooms or furniture in this place! The rooms and halls, if that's what they were, could have been any shape.

"What's wrong with my eyes here, White? All the lines run together here."

"What you see here has higher vibrations, Michael Thomas, and your mind is not able to make much sense of it right now. That is why I did not meet you at the door. I cannot go out-side of this place. My vibration follows the rules for being inside this house, which are not the same as the rules for being outside of it."

Mike didn't know enough about this to ask any more questions. He followed White to a door he thought he'd seen before, one he could see clearly.

"Your bedroom and dining room are in your vibration, Michael, so I cannot go in with you. I'll be just outside the door here, though, to greet you every morning after breakfast."

There was something about White's voice that made Mike want to hear it over and over. It was beautiful! He remembered how he'd reacted to White's laughter the first time he'd heard it. He never wanted White to leave. "Do you have to go?"

"Yes, but only for now. I'll be here in the morning."

"I'll miss you." Mike felt as if he were saying good-bye to someone very, very close to him, like his mother or father. He wanted to keep feeling the energy they shared together and real-ized that this was very different.

White knew what question was coming. "White, what is it I'm feeling? Can you explain it to me so I can understand?"

"No." White was honest and smiled at Mike. "But I'll tell you anyway." This magnificent angel was more than happy to talk about everything, even if it was over Mike's head spiritually. "I represent the source for all that is. I represent all light. I am the space between the nucleus of the atom and its electrons. There is more of my force than any other force in the Universe, and my energy is the strongest. I am each tick of the clock, yet I am the center, where there is no time. I am the creative force that allows energy to become knowledge; therefore, I am a miracle. I AM Love."

The message was hard to understand, but awesome anyway. Mike almost felt like he was standing in front of God. This angel was no simple teacher. He was very holy, and had the most wonderful voice he'd ever heard. Mike had felt this way the first time they'd met. "Thank you, White, thank you."

White looked at Mike for a very long time before he spoke again. The angel's silky voice was like the morning sun over the trees. "You will not spend much time here, Michael Thomas. Tomorrow I'll explain what love really is, and then there is someone I would like you to meet."

White left, leaving Mike wishing for more of everything: more of that wonderful voice, more answers to his questions, more of that peaceful feeling!

Mike had forgotten how hungry he was until he smelled the food in the other room. He quickly put his things in the closet and washed up. After dinner, Mike slept better than ever. Whatever he'd experienced in the other houses, this was better. The peacefulness he was experiencing here was so strong he could just about taste and smell it.

✳   ✳   ✳

When the gross red-eyed creature finally came upon the White House, it didn't stop to hide behind a tree or wait behind a rock. IT knew that it could sneak past the little house without being seen, since Mike was already inside. A dark purpose drove

IT ahead on the road toward the next house. IT found the perfect place down the road for its attack. There was no way that Mike could escape from its trap. With all the details wrapped up, IT then made itself comfortable, waiting and practicing the plan. *The trap is perfect,* IT thought. *There's no way puny little Michael Thomas can win—tricking him will be no problem.*

The sun was setting, and if you'd been a traveler on that road where IT had set the trap, you'd have only seen what appeared to be a boy standing under a tree all by himself, saying the same words over and over, as if he were practicing a speech. And if you'd come closer to the boy, you'd have seen his gentle face and heard his friendly voice—it was Michael Thomas's best buddy, Bryan.

* * *

Mike woke up early and got himself ready. His rooms were like those in the other houses except that they were completely white. All of the white here made him feel very peaceful and calm. He found some clothes and slippers to wear—white, of course.

He ate—and what a meal! It not only tasted good, it looked good. The table was set beautifully with a white tablecloth and white dishes; there were white cups and glasses and even white forks and knives. All that white made the food look like a beautiful painting. Mike ate slowly, feeling like he was eating in a mansion or a palace.

When he'd finished eating, Mike took a deep breath. He knew that the grand, white angel was just on the other side of the door, waiting. *What's going to happen here? If love is the greatest power in the Universe, and my vibrations are getting higher and stronger toward that love, then what could be bad enough to stop my journey?*

Mike opened his door and stepped into the delicate hallway of the White House. There was the gorgeous white angel, just like he said he'd be, waiting for him right where Mike had left him the night before.

"Good morning, Michael Thomas," said the cheerful angel. Mike immediately felt the grandness of the energy around White.

"And good morning to you, White."

"Are you ready to move forward?"

"Ready as I'll ever be," Mike replied.

White led him into a white room and asked him to sit down. There were no pointers, screens, or charts here; it was empty except for one chair for Mike. Mike sat down in the chair, and the angel began teaching.

"Michael Thomas of Pure Intent, I am here to explain to you the truth about love. When the pure love of God vibrates throughout your whole body, each one of your cells will vibrate with that love.

Everything will seem different to you. You will treat others differently. You will be very wise. Love is the center of everything, yet amazingly enough, your language has only one word for it!" The angel smiled. "I wish to show you how love really works. Please, come with me."

Mike was surprised by what happened next. He thought he'd been through a lot in the first six houses and had seen everything, but suddenly the angel was taking him on a little trip! He was whooshed into another place, still sitting in his chair. He and White seemed real enough, but everything else felt like a dream. He was moving, but he wasn't dizzy at all. The white, blurry room became full of colors and sounds, changing before Mike's eyes. He was being taken somewhere else, and although he was surprised, he wasn't afraid.

After a few minutes, he and White finally came to the place the angel had in mind. As everything settled, Mike could see that

they were in a hospital room. This was surprising—Mike thought White was taking him to some heavenly place to look at the love of God. Instead, here he was, looking at a regular old hospital room where a sick person was lying in bed. From the looks of it, that person was very, very ill.

It was so real! Mike could hear everything as it was happening, and he could actually smell all the hospital smells! Floating high up in the corner, he and White were where they could see everything that was going on in the room. Nothing was moving; only the beeping, hissing, and clicking of the hospital equipment could be heard. Mike looked around. The man in the bed had his eyes closed, and he looked very pale, very old, and very sick.

"What's wrong with him?" Mike quietly asked White, as if the sick man might hear him.

"He is dying," replied White.

Mike started to ask another question when a woman about the same age as his mom came into the hospital room. She was alone. She stood there for a few minutes just inside the room, looking at the man in the bed. Mike's intuition told him she was special—his intuition was strong, even here in what seemed like a dream. "Who is she?"

"Her name is Mary. The dying man is her father. But what you are seeing here is really about her. She has every reason to hate the man in that bed."

"Why should she hate her father?"

"Because he was so mean to her when she was just a child. He drank too much and stayed drunk most of the time. He yelled at Mary and sometimes hit her when her mother was not at home. It really hurt her and made her think that every father was as terrible as hers. It ruined her life." White paused, and they both watched Mary go up to the bed.

The angel went on. "Mary moved away as soon as she finished school to get away from her father. Her mother never knew anything about it because Mary was too afraid to tell her. They could never be friends because her mother thought that Mary didn't want *her.* Even when Mary got older, she still could not tell her, so her mother died thinking that her own daughter did not love her."

"That's awful!" Mike thought this was so unfair and felt very sorry for Mary. And her mother, too.

The angel looked at Mike with puzzlement. "They are *family,* Michael. Surely you have not already forgotten the lessons you learned at the Red House?"

Mike felt ashamed. No, he hadn't forgotten, but it was hard to remember to use his new knowledge about his own spiritual family to try to understand another person's situation. He realized that White was hinting that the father and daughter had made a contract together and had planned their lives together—just as Mike and his family had.

"It gets worse, Michael. Mary had hoped to find someone special and fall in love. But each time she met someone, she just knew each man she met would drink whiskey all the time and yell and hit. She never was able to settle down and have a family of her own."

Mike sighed, then spoke. "Gosh, that was some contract." He really felt sorry for Mary, and could hardly imagine how difficult life had been for her.

The angel looked at Mike with pride and admiration.

"Do you understand, Michael Thomas, that what happened with Mary and her father was a contract of incredible love?"

"I do, White, but it's still hard."

"That is because you are a young human trying to think in a God-like way, and it takes some getting used to. You may never fully understand some of these things so long as you are human, and that is okay. You will, eventually."

Mike kept looking at Mary and her dying father. Mary was staring quietly at him, maybe waiting for him to wake up. She put some of her things on the table by the bed. "She must hate him very much," Mike said sadly and softly to White.

"No, Michael. She loves him greatly."

This was certainly a shock! "After everything he did to her?"

White turned toward him. "Mary shares something with you, Michael Thomas." The angel stopped and looked hard at Mike to see how he was taking this. "Like you, she has learned all the lessons you have so far—what's different is that she learned them on Earth."

Mike was amazed! He thought that a human could only be trained in spiritual things in the angel houses. He didn't know what to say. *How could this be?*

The angel saw that Mike was confused and continued. "Mary made all her changes on her own, Michael, and it took almost nine years of her life. You have made your changes in only a few weeks! You are indeed special. All of what you have learned in the angel houses has been out there for humans to learn on Earth all this time. Humans have to realize that they are human, but that there is also a spark of God in them. They must make up their minds to learn all they can about the truth of spiritual things. Many books have been written about how these spiritual things work, and there are many human teachers who can help."

Mike was very quiet. He was thinking about something that had been bothering him since he visited the Violet House. *Did I make a mistake right after the accident by asking White to allow me to leave Earth and go Home?* But Mike did not ask White this question yet. He was not sure that he really wanted to know the answer. Instead, his thoughts turned back to Mary.

"White, why did it take her nine years?"

"She took her time, Michael, and was honored for it. She was not lucky enough to have all the angels who taught you. She did not have the honor, as you did, of meeting her spiritual family face to face. She doesn't know their angel names like you do. It took much longer for her to learn and understand since she is still in the Earth vibration and lives within that energy."

Mike sat and looked at Mary. Here she was, so spiritually advanced, but she looked so small and delicate.

"Don't let that fool you, Michael. Not everything is as it seems." The white angel had read his energy again. "She is a Warrior of the Light. She has killed the giant and is powerful!"

Mike was really starting to feel uncomfortable now. *What exactly does that mean?* He was about to ask when White spoke again.

"Michael Thomas of Pure Intent, we are here so that one who looks like an ordinary woman can teach you the truth about love."

Mike was very still. He felt that there was so very much to learn. Just when he was getting closer to Home, things were getting tougher.

The angel continued. "Pay attention, for Mary carries with her the same power that I do. She truly understands love, Michael, and because of that, a part of me lives in her. There is no greater power than this."

Mike watched Mary while White went on to explain what was going on.

"Michael Thomas, watching Mary is a wonderful way to learn about love. What she does here will show you the four characteristics or attributes of love, the first being this: LOVE IS QUIET. You saw that Mary came into her father's room quietly. She could have come in making a big deal about everything that happened in the past, to get him back for what he did to her. Her father is so ill, there would be nothing he could do about it. He knows what he did, Michael, and he is ashamed and guilty. His life was hard, too, and he has not handled it well. He doesn't know the spiritual things Mary knows. He doesn't have her new power. Watch her quietness, Michael Thomas."

They watched as Mary straightened her father's sheets. She sat beside the sick man and lay her head gently on his chest. Mike could feel what she was feeling! Somehow White was allowing for this. Mary was very peaceful and calm. There wasn't a single thought about getting her father back. She'd forgiven him so completely that she didn't have a problem with what happened before. It just didn't bother her now. She wasn't even angry. Mike felt her feelings of love toward this man who'd carried out his part of their plan so completely and had such a serious effect on her life.

It took a long time, but finally the father opened his eyes and saw that she was there. She stood when he woke up. His eyes got very big, and for a minute he was surprised and very afraid of how she'd act. Here she was! What was she doing here? He hadn't seen her in so long! Would she scream at him for all the pain he had caused her? The hospital equipment started beeping a lot faster.

"Watch, Michael," White spoke in his wonderful flowing voice. "Here now is the second attribute of love: LOVE DOESN'T EXPECT CERTAIN THINGS TO HAPPEN. Mary could ask her father now for anything she wants, because he is so weak and feels guilty about what he has done. He is a very rich man. She could expect him to pay her back for all her hurting, or maybe she could just make him apologize for all that he did. Watch her, Michael."

Mary placed her hand on her father's head and whispered in his ear. Immediately, the hospital machines got quieter. He sighed, and Mike could see tears start in his eyes. "What did she say, White?" Mike didn't hear Mary's whisper.

"She said, *I love you, father, and I forgive you completely.*"

Mike was amazed at how serious all this was. He wondered if he would have been strong enough and wise enough to do the same if that were him. He admired Mary very much. "She didn't ask for anything?"

"No, Michael. She is content to simply *be.*"

Again, Mike felt what Mary felt. Everything between Mary and her father in the plan was over and done now. Mary was at peace. She'd also just released something that her father had been sad about for many, many years! You could see it in his face. Instead of being mean and expecting to be paid back, Mary had given her father a *gift*. Now big tears were flowing down his cheeks. Mary again sat and wrapped her arms around this precious man, and again lay her head on his chest. There was no talking. It wasn't needed.

"Michael Thomas, the third attribute of love is this: LOVE DOESN'T PUFF ITSELF UP. Now that Mary has proven that her wisdom and understanding are glorious indeed, she doesn't say anything. Her father owes her so much for her forgiveness, yet she remains quiet. She could have stood tall—puffed up with power and pride that she was able to forgive him—yet she remains quiet."

This woman truly amazed Mike. She was indeed a Warrior of the Light, and understood things that Mike was just now learning. Imagine—she was still on Earth with all this knowledge! *What a peaceful and happy life she must have,* Mike thought. He couldn't take his eyes off of all that was happening.

There was nothing the father could say. All had been forgiven, and he felt a wonderful peace as he let go of the past. Mary's vibration changed because of how she'd handled herself. Mike knew that he was witnessing something very important here.

Mary's father took a long look at his wonderful daughter and gently closed his eyes. The smile on his face was one of pure peace. Mary had given him the most important gift of his life— just in time. The hospital machines sounded in alarm, and the quiet hissing stopped. Mike knew that Mary's father had just passed on. Hospital workers rushed into the room, but there was nothing to be done. They turned off the machines, covered his head, and left him alone with his daughter.

"Michael Thomas, the fourth attribute of love is this: LOVE HAS THE WISDOM TO USE THE OTHER THREE ATTRIBUTES PER-FECTLY! Mary did not have a map like yours, Michael Thomas, but she used her *feelings* as a map to help her to do everything in perfect time. Now watch what she does."

Mike turned back to look at Mary. She wasn't crying her heart out because her father was gone, even though she loved him very much. She asked the hospital workers to let her stay in the room for a while more. Mike watched as Mary put her hand on her father's chest—this was the man who'd brought her into this world. She lifted up her head and faced White and Mike! She seemed to speak right to them! Mike heard Mary's strong voice for the first time.

"Let Earth remember this man, whom I love dearly." Mary's voice was firm as she went on. "He came and did just as he and I planned. I accept his gift! Honor his return Home."

Mary lowered her eyes, gathered her things, and quietly left the room. Mike's mouth was wide open. He almost couldn't believe what he'd just seen. The moment was intense. He'd just watched a contract being completed, and what a finish!

"It was the wisdom of love that let Mary be happy about her father's death. There was no need for her to be sad. What do you feel, Michael Thomas of Pure Intent?" White waited quietly for Mike to think this over.

"I feel . . . " Mike had to clear his throat. "I feel . . . that I've learned more from Mary than I have from all the angels so far." Then Mike realized what he had said, and he was embarrassed. "Not that I don't appreciate—"

White held up his hand and stopped Mike. "Your answer was perfect, Michael Thomas. Perfect. It is the human who has shown you more clearly what the angels have been trying to teach you. That is as it should be and as it will be in the next test as well."

Instantly the hospital room got blurry, and again Mike felt as if he were moving. Before long they were back where they'd started in the White House. Mike was very quiet.

"Do you have any questions, Michael Thomas?"

Mike thought about what he really wanted. He knew that Mary was stronger than he was. He knew that even though he'd learned so much from the angels, he still didn't have the power Mary had. Mike had tools, a wonderful map, and much knowledge; he had a high vibration and had been through a lot, but he didn't have the love that Mary had. Then he asked the big question: "Can I have this powerful love, too, White?"

"Is it your intent that it be so, Michael?"

"Yes, it is."

"Michael Thomas of Pure Intent, do you love God?"

Mike stood up very straight, thinking that this must be why all the angels asked him this question—for this very moment—so that he could stand here and answer. "Yes, I do, White." He was very proper.

"Then let your pure intent create the power!"

Mike didn't remember what happened next. It was like he fainted. He had dreams . . . he was being carried somewhere . . . there was a ceremony . . . there was a celebration . . . something was given to him . . . a gift that he could carry in all the cells of his body. There were his people again! It was all so fuzzy. And so wonderful.

When he woke up, he was on his white bed, in his white room. It was evening, and Mike was worn out. His mind was foggy and he couldn't think straight. *What happened?* He'd figure it all out later. Now he needed rest. Mike crawled under the covers and fell asleep right away. As before, he slept very well.

* * *

When he woke up the next morning, Mike felt as if he'd gone through another change in his vibration. He sat on the edge of his bed for a very long time, thinking about it. He felt rested and peaceful and new! He couldn't tell exactly what had happened, but whatever it was, he felt wiser. But he also felt troubled.

Mike couldn't stop thinking about Mary and her father. Mary was on Earth, yet she'd made great changes in her vibration and was powerful in her life. She hadn't asked to go Home. She'd suffered through her life on Earth and stuck with it. But Mike had given up! Where was the honor there?

Mike's new wisdom was starting to make him think twice about everything. He was starting to understand what Red and White might have meant about his choice to continue on his journey. Was he doing the right thing? Was there more to this journey than what he had asked for?

Mike continued to think about all of this as he dressed and ate his breakfast. He wanted to ask White what he should do.

White was waiting, as usual, on the other side of the door. Mike stepped closer to the angel, but was too stunned to speak. He stared at his surroundings in disbelief. All the fuzziness of the white walls and floors and hallways had disappeared! Everything was now crystal clear! He saw tiny details all around that he hadn't been able to see before. It was beautiful!

"It is your new sight, Michael Thomas," said the angel, knowing what Mike was feeling. "Your vibration has changed again. Now it is the same as Mary's, because you have intended it so purely. We don't see such a pure intention very often."

"I have to ask you some important questions, White." Mike was shocked by how his own voice sounded! It was bigger than it should have been—or was it louder? He couldn't tell. He only knew that it didn't sound like *him*.

"Michael, be still for a moment," the angel said gently. "Your intent to go ahead on this journey means that many things about you will change. Yesterday you chose to make the biggest change in yourself yet. You will change more and more on the road ahead, Michael. The way you see, the sound of your voice, and your very thoughts. You are turning into a Warrior of the Light—just like Mary."

Mike felt a rush of understanding and wisdom as he listened to White's words. "Thank you, White. I understand. But I feel that I still need to talk to you about some things. I need your help."

"There is much I can tell you, Michael, and I'll tell you whatever I can. But you are wise enough now to make your own choices. They are for you alone to make."

Mike knew from his journey so far that the angels weren't going to do the work for him. He knew that the lessons were for *him* to learn.

"You're a great teacher, White." Mike's voice still sounded different. It reminded him of hearing himself recorded on a tape recorder for the first time. *Is that really what I sound like?*

White motioned for Mike to follow him down the hall. It was like being given a tour of an entirely new house. Everything around Mike was beautiful and new, like a king's palace. *What else have I been missing?* Mike wondered.

"The colors, Michael," White answered Mike without even turning around. "You don't see the colors yet."

"But this is the WHITE House," Mike said as they moved ahead. The angel laughed, filling the hallways and making Mike smile.

"Only to your human eyes, Michael. The actual color of love is far greater than the vibration that you can see and feel now. You see white because the other vibrations are out of your range. Actually, white glows with all the other colors together. It is pure, and is at the top of the color range. Its light is so strong that you can see it and feel it. It is a billion times brighter than the Sun. It is the color of Truth. There is much you cannot see with your human eyes."

"I love this place!" exclaimed Mike.

"We shall see if you still feel that way later," said White.

That sure doesn't sound good! Mike thought. Now he had more questions, but he continued down the dazzling hallways behind White until they came to a stark white room. There were windows, but again, there was no furniture except for one small chair in the middle of the room.

"Another journey, White?"

"Not exactly, Michael. But it will take you somewhere. Please sit down."

Mike did as the angel asked. Folding his hands, White spoke again. "Michael Thomas of Pure Intent, what is it you wish to know?"

Mike was ready. "White, you know so much. Could you please tell me . . . did I make a mistake by choosing to go Home?"

White was quiet for a moment. "I told you from the start that what you were doing was right for *you.* And we would not support you in something that was *not* correct for you."

"But Mary?" Mike blurted out. "She had all the gifts and tools but stayed on Earth. Isn't that what I should have done? Wouldn't that have been a more spiritual thing to do?"

"For *her*," replied a wise White.

"But I feel like I'm being selfish, White! I'm going Home to where love is. How does this help anyone else besides me? It doesn't seem to help anyone still on Earth."

"Seem?" White interrupted.

"Yes. It SEEMS selfish." Mike was upset. He sat silently.

"What did I tell you when we first met, Michael, about the way things *seem*?" White was testing Mike.

"That things are not always as they seem." Mike had heard that again and again on this journey—both Blue and Violet had reminded him of it.

"Very good!" said White. "What else?"

Mike couldn't remember.

The angel continued. "Your wish for Home is normal, not selfish." He paused. "Now that you have made it this far, I'll tell you one other thing." The grand angel lowered his voice. "There is a wonderful new energy on the Earth, which will make it much easier for great things to happen now. You are here because of that new energy, so new that only a few humans have been able to journey this far. You are one of the first, Michael Thomas. That is why we are so happy that you have learned so much here."

Mike was quiet for a long time. Finally, he spoke. "Okay, so it's all right that I'm here. But really, White, would it have been better to stay on Earth? To do what Mary did? I mean, where should I really be? What could I do that would be best for everyone? That's my real question."

White swelled up even bigger, he was so proud of Mike. Then he spoke seriously. "When this question is asked, Michael Thomas, it shows that you truly are starting to understand the way things work. Your wisdom is starting to show, Michael."

"Thank you, White, but what's the answer?" Mike appreciated the compliment, but he just had to know the answer to his question. He hoped he wasn't being too pushy.

"The best for everyone?" White began to move away. "It is your own life, Michael, and you have changed so much now that you can make it be what you need it to be. No one else can do that for you."

Mike saw that this was the end of the discussion. Some questions didn't have simple answers. "White, will I ever know what's best for everyone?"

"What happens next will help you answer your own question." White floated toward the door, leaving Mike alone in the center of the room. "You do not have all the information yet, Michael. This is the House of Love. There is still more for you to see here. And Michael," the angel said as he moved into the hallway, "it gets harder now."

White left and the door closed silently. Mike heard the click of the latch, and all was still. He knew that something was coming, something big. But he was patient. He realized that whatever was going to happen would happen, without White. It was something that Mike had to go through by himself. Either he'd learned his lessons or he hadn't.

The whole room seemed to change slowly, and the light looked different. Everything started to get blurry. A few feet in front of Mike, a fuzzy cloud started glowing. Then the cloud began to change its shape—it looked like a person! Mike sat up straight in his chair. He knew he was about to meet someone; White had told him so. But who? The figure continued to form, and the light behind it got brighter. Every cell in his body told him that this was a big deal. His intuition told him the same. The image finally formed. His visitor appeared . . .

A woman!

Standing before Mike was a lady so beautiful that he couldn't breathe. Her red hair flowed around her perfect face. She smiled at Mike, and his heart just about jumped out of his chest. Her sparkling eyes were as green as four-leaf clovers. The scent of flowers filled the room. All kinds of things went through Mike's mind. *Is this the Goddess of Love I read about in the old fairy tales?* He looked at the woman in amazement.

Mike had seen angels along the way, but if this lady was an angel, then she had to be the grandest of them all. *Is she the one White was talking about when he told me that there was an even grander angel coming?* Mike couldn't speak. His heart felt as if it were connected to hers, as if he knew her well. It was crazy. He was just a kid, but he felt he'd loved her before. The room was all clear now, and as she stood in front of him, Mike decided that she had to be the most beautiful thing he'd ever seen.

Then Mike realized that he *had* seen that beautiful face before. He recognized her! She was one of the people in his family chart in the Red House that he hadn't gotten to meet. She was what Red had called one of the "unfulfilled contracts." What had Red meant? Mike didn't know what to say. Luckily, the red-haired woman spoke first.

"Mike, it's me."

He'd heard that voice before. *How? Who is she?* Her eyes were begging Mike to remember her. He knew her from the chart in the Red House, but not from anything else that he could be sure of. Mike had to speak. His heart was beating so fast, and he couldn't quit thinking about how wonderful it would be to marry her later when he became a man. What in the world was the *matter* with him?

"You're so beautiful."

It just squeaked out. He was really embarrassed. There he was, a kid with a squeak for a voice in a mighty land of angels, thinking about marrying this woman.

"I am Anolee. If you'd stayed on Earth, there was a good chance that we would have met. We planned it together, remember? We had a contract." Mike didn't remember, and he didn't want to hear about how he'd missed out on this. The lady saw how sad this made him.

"It's okay," she said. "I'm here to tell you that what you're doing is honored. It's all right. Really. The family is proud, and we're all very happy about it. Especially me."

But Mike was still disappointed. His parents were so loving toward each other, and he'd hoped that when it came time for him to get married, he and his wife could be like that, too. He hadn't really spent a lot of time thinking about it, though. He was just a kid, after all. But looking at this beautiful woman now, and feeling the way he did about her, he wished that he could marry her someday. But he'd chosen to go Home, instead. *I left too soon!*

Then he had a really weird thought. "Would we have had any kids, Anolee?"

"There were to have been three," she replied.

Mike suddenly realized all that he was going to miss out on. *What have I done?* he thought.

Mike wanted to hold Anolee's hand and tell her how sorry he was that he hadn't stayed, even though she was there to support his decision to go Home. Tears began to roll down his cheeks.

Anolee stood quietly in front of Michael Thomas. It was pitiful. There he was, sitting in front of the most beautiful woman he'd ever seen, and all he could do was sit and cry like a little boy. He was crushed that he'd given up on her and their life together.

Then Anolee started to disappear. "No! *Please* don't go! PLEASE!" Mike felt he'd never see her again.

"Michael, things are not necessarily what they seem." Now *she* was saying it! By the time the words were spoken, Anolee had returned to a glowing ball of light. The light slowly faded until it disappeared altogether.

Mike didn't move from his chair for hours. He stared at the spot where Anolee had stood, hoping that she'd come back and he could have just a few more minutes with her.

The room grew dim as the sun went down. Finally, it was dark . . . like Mike's heart. He'd come so far in his journey, but now he felt as if he'd just gone back to being the same unhappy kid he was before he began down the path. *I would have had a wonderful life with Anolee when I got older, but that's all gone now. This is worse than losing Bryan.* Losing so much was exhausting, and Mike fell into a deep sleep right there in his chair. He had dream after dream about Anolee.

Mike's heart was broken.

$$* \quad * \quad *$$

The light of the new day filled the room and woke Mike up. He was aching all over from sleeping in the stiff chair. He knew that he needed to eat, but he just wasn't hungry. He forced himself to get up, and he went to his dining room. Even though all of his favorite breakfast foods were on the table, Mike just ate like a robot. His stomach was full, but his heart was empty. He went to his room and opened the closet. There, right where he'd left them, were all his gifts from the angels, given to him with love.

In all of his sadness, Mike remembered his earlier question to White: *Will I ever know what I could do that would be best for everyone?* Now he understood the test. He wanted so badly to go back

to Earth right now. All he had to do was walk out of the house and turn left on the road instead of right. He knew it. The angels would see that he'd changed his mind and had decided to go back. White had told him that he could change his mind at any time and there would be no problem—but there would be no more lessons taught by the angels, either.

Mike *did* know what to do, what would be the best for everyone. Anolee had told him that his family was proud of him, and he realized that *her* heart probably hurt, too. Yet she'd encouraged him to go on with his journey. She was letting him make his own choice. Mike was finally understanding the true meaning of love.

Mike picked up his map and held it close, thinking back to his time in the Blue House. He slowly put on his armor and felt its power as he blessed it and thanked God for the precious wisdom it stood for. He picked up the shield and held it against his chest with both hands, thinking about what it meant to him. Then he strapped it on his back so it would be there when he needed it. He lifted his sword and thought of what it represented, and then he blessed it and slid it into its holder. Mike stood tall in his handsome traveling clothes, and then left his room, ready for action.

White was there when Mike came out of his room. The angel saw the armor, shield, and sword and knew right then what Mike was going to do. White smiled and bowed low, with his hands together like he was praying—Mike didn't realize how much honor the angel was showing him.

"Michael Thomas of Pure Intent, how do you feel?"

"This is hard for me, White. You were right. I didn't know how hard it would be to learn this house's lessons. Please, White, I want to leave your beautiful house. It's just too sad for me here, and I have something important to do."

"So it shall be." White turned and led Mike toward the door. The angel spoke to Mike over his shoulder as he led the way. "Your journey is not over, my little human friend." White was now floating down the grand hallway that led to the front door.

"I know." Mike's intuition told him that there was still much to see and learn and do, even though there was only one house left. He hadn't liked the White House very much, just as White had warned him when he had first arrived.

White stood just inside the door while Mike put on his shoes. He knew what Mike was feeling, but he was still very proud of the boy. The other angels had been right. Mike was different. He would make it Home if he survived the last part of his journey. His wisdom and his determination were great.

Mike took a few steps out into the yard, then turned around and faced the angel.

White spoke to him from the doorway. "Michael Thomas of Pure Intent, there is no greater love than this . . . that a human would give up what he wants the most in order to do what he has to do." White smiled at Mike. As the door swung shut, Mike could hear the angel's final words. "Not everything is as it seems. You will see. You will see. You are dearly loved . . . "

Mike walked down the little path to the road. This had not been his favorite house, and he was getting tired of hearing that *not everything is as it seems.* Almost every angel had reminded him of that. The White House had taken a lot out of him, but he wouldn't realize until later that he'd actually taken a lot from it, too. He stood for a long time at the white gate, looking left, then right down the road. Finally, he walked through the gate to the middle of the road. He turned left, closed his eyes, and started praying. He knew that the angels would be listening.

"I'm not really giving anything up here, because we will meet again, Anolee. When the time comes, we'll be together, when I reach the door to Home." Mike finally understood what the angels had tried to teach him about life on Earth lasting only for a short time, and how life in the Spirit was forever. He started to see that while he didn't get to know Anolee on Earth, he would get to be with her and the rest of his spiritual family at Home.

Then Mike sighed and turned back to the right to continue his journey to the last house. His armor softly clanked around him as he walked in the sunshine. The White House had taught him the most about himself—and God. But he didn't look back this time. He walked like a warrior and felt powerful and safe. This was his land now. He had certainly earned it. He deserved it.

Mike would soon find his power challenged, for a short way up the road another great test awaited Michael Thomas . . . the battle for his very soul.

* * * * * *

Chapter Eleven

The Seventh House

Down the road a bit, Mike noticed that the weather was changing. His experience in this land so far had told him that the day would either be wonderful and sunshiny or horrible and stormy. But today was unusual. The sky was covered over in dark clouds that made everything look gray. The air was cool, too. There was a little breeze that came in waves, as if it was trying to tell him something. The clouds didn't get any worse as he went on, but they looked as if they were there to stay. Mike wasn't worried about the weather but decided to be careful just the same.

Mike walked like a robot, thinking about his choice to stay on his journey. He couldn't stop thinking about what it could have been like when he got older—being married to Anolee and having a family like his mother and father had. The thought of such a life made his heart feel light. Being with Bryan and winning the big game had never felt this good. But when he looked ahead on the road and saw it wind toward the unknown, Mike felt all alone and very sad. Still, he walked forward, not noticing that the land was slowly changing and was becoming quite different.

The road led Mike into a canyon with sides that went straight up to the sky. He finally saw that there were no more gentle hills and soft grass. Everything now looked like a desert with huge rocks and dirt— and very few trees. How bare everything looked! Mike realized that he'd been thinking so hard that he hadn't noticed where it had changed. With the high canyon walls and gray clouds surrounding him and blocking any sunlight, Mike thought it looked more like sunset than early morning.

The grayness of everything made Mike feel really sleepy. But he suddenly snapped out of it and took several deep breaths to clear his mind. He was being "poked" by his intuition. His body tingled. What did it mean? *Something must be wrong up ahead.* Mike obeyed his intuition and looked all around for trouble. He searched the road behind him, trying to find the terrible creature that had been following him each time he got out on the road. But nothing was moving. Mike's intuition still told him to be ready for anything, and he softly thanked his new vibratory power for doing its job. He took out his map—maybe *it* would tell him something.

As usual, the map showed the area immediately around Mike—in this case, the canyon he was in—but there was something different. He looked closer. There! About a hundred yards up the road on the map, just out of sight from where Mike actually stood, was a blank spot. Usually the map was filled in around the red *"You Are Here"* dot, and he could trust it to be accurate and truthful in every beautiful detail. He decided he'd better ask what the deal was with this blank spot.

"Blue, what does a blank spot on the map mean?"

Blue didn't answer, but Mike's own intuition did, almost immediately. He remembered that the thing that had been following him stayed just far enough away not to show up on the map. Maybe because IT knew it would appear on the map—as a blank spot!

Blue had told Mike that the map could only show what was happening right now. That meant that there was something ahead that didn't belong in the Now. Something not visible to the map's high energy, which wasn't vibrating the same as the sacred land around it. IT didn't belong here.

Mike was sure he'd figured this out correctly—the thing was waiting for him ahead on the path. But Mike felt the peace and power of his choice to go Home. He was waking up each cell in his body with the message that something very important was about to happen.

"Wake up, everyone!" Mike smiled as he thought about talking to his body like this, and again he thought he could hear Green laughing. He missed Green—it was he who had taught Mike that laughter felt good. But how tough would things get now? Could there really be . . . a battle?

Suddenly, like a huge ocean wave of understanding, thoughts and pictures came crashing down on Mike. He realized what was happening! "I'm not really supposed to USE these weapons!" He was really starting to be upset. "These are just symbols that stand for the truth, knowledge, and wisdom used by a Warrior of the Light! SYMBOLS!" he yelled. Mike looked up at the sky to see if any of his angel friends were leaning against the walls of the canyon in the dim light. But his only answer was his voice echoing back at him.

"Orange, you never taught me how to fight! So I thought I would never have to really use—," Mike stopped in mid-sentence, realizing that he was shouting. Then words he'd heard along the way started coming back to him. Red had said that some of the tests would scare him, but he just thought Red was talking about the terrible storm. Now he realized that Red was talking about things to come, not things that had already happened. What in the world was he about to face?

Then Mike remembered what White had said about Mary in the hospital room. *"Don't let looks fool you, Michael. She's a Warrior of the Light. She's slain the giant and is powerful!"* Slain the giant? Then White's warning came back to him: *"Your journey is not over, my little human friend."*

All these warnings and hints. Mike's knees began to shake, so he sat down on the road. He wasn't a warrior—not a *real* one! He was just a little kid!

"Angels, you didn't teach me about this!" he said to the sky. "I don't want to really fight! Why would this happen? You taught me that real battles and real weapons are old energy things. They don't belong here!" There was an odd stillness: The wind had stopped blowing and it was deathly quiet. Then the voices started.

"Unless you are about to fight an old energy." He heard the clear voice of Orange and instantly stood up and twirled around to see where the voice was coming from.

"And unless you're about to fight a creature that doesn't vibrate as high as you do." That was Green! The angels' voices were coming from inside him.

"And unless who you're about to meet really isn't part of your family, Michael." Now Red had spoken!

"And unless there is no love there, Michael." It was the soft and wonderful voice of White!

"I DIDN'T KNOW!" cried a worried Michael Thomas. "I'm not a real warrior, White!"

"Neither was Mary, Michael." White's words were comforting.

"The old energy follows the old rules, Michael. That is what it understands." It was Violet's lovely, warm voice!

"Orange, tell me how to fight!" Mike was trying not to panic.

"I did." Orange's voice was encouraging. *"You're ready, Michael Thomas of Pure Intent. Believe me, you're ready."*

"What should I do?" Mike cried.

Silence. Then Blue's voice. *"Remember, Michael Thomas, things may not be as they seem!"*

The words rang out like they never had before. They sounded out a warning and advice that Mike needed right now! All of the angels were with him.

Mike was nervous. He knew that he didn't actually know how to fight a battle, and yet the angels were telling him that he did. He had to trust them, and after all, what choice did he have now? He was on the battlefield. He looked around and thought, *There's no way to get out of here.* Whatever or whoever was waiting for him had picked a good place to attack. The sides of the canyon were too steep to climb, and the only way out was a narrow passage between the high walls—Mike would be easy prey. Everything had been carefully thought out. At least, thanks to the blank spot on his map, he knew where IT was, and there'd be no surprises.

But the more Mike thought about it all, the more confident he became. His new vibration was helping out, and he knew it. It was crazy, but he was feeling peaceful in the middle of all this. He was beginning to feel powerful and ready for action, even though he didn't know exactly what he was facing, or how he would fight IT. *That makes sense,* Mike thought. *After all, that's how things work here. I don't know the future, but somehow it's already happened in the mind of God. So, the answer to this is already out there. I just don't know it yet. Like before at the fork in the road, I'll know when I get there. I have the knowledge and the power, and this is my land. I belong here, IT doesn't, so everything is going for me!*

"Okay," Mike said out loud. "I've been beaten up by a storm, had my toe stomped by an angel, lost my gym bag and all my best stuff . . . what else is there? I have the tools. I'm ready." Mike thought for a minute, then muttered, "I just wish I knew how to fight!"

Mike then decided to do something that a few weeks ago would have seemed silly. He knelt down and held a little ceremony over what was about to happen. He touched the sword with love, remembering that it stood for truth. He touched the shield and armor with love, remembering that they stood for knowledge and wisdom. He drilled himself with the things Orange had taught him about balance. He spent almost 20 minutes in thanks for being chosen to battle whatever was around the corner. He honored the land and his being there. He thought of his place in the family of Spirit; then Michael Thomas got up, ready for bat-tle—as ready as he could be, anyway.

Mike started forward again. He went around a corner and looked down the long, dark road ahead. The high walls of the canyon made it look like a tunnel of doom. He knew IT was ahead. The old Michael would have gone into shock by now. But every part of the new Michael was paying careful attention, and he was determined, not fearful. All of his vibratory powers and new gifts were starting to work. Mike's intuition was running the show, and with each step, he listened to it, knowing that it wouldn't let him down.

Something moved to the left!

Mike turned quickly and saw a large tree close by the roadside. But he didn't notice anything unusual. *It's too hard to see in this dim light! Is this part of the test? Why hasn't Spirit sent more light?*

There was the motion again! Mike saw that it came from just under the branches of the tree. "WHO'S THERE? COME OUT!" Mike's voice was loud and powerful. "IF YOU DON'T COME OUT, I'M COMING IN!" He stood waiting, every cell in his body on full alert.

Slowly, a regular-looking boy stepped out from behind the tree and stopped just under the outer branches. He was dressed in regular clothes. He held up his hands with his palms turned toward Mike and spoke. "Hey, Mike, please don't hurt me! I'll come out."

The boy slowly walked toward the road. As he got closer, Mike could see him better and thought he recognized him. *No! It can't be! What's going on here?* "Bryan?"

Bryan slowly walked up the road and stood right in front of Mike. "Yep, Ace, it's me. Please—don't hurt me."

But Mike was no dummy. He knew that this could be a trick, even though Bryan always used to call him Ace. *After all, things are not always as they seem.* The boy who looked like Bryan could actually be something else; in fact, it was a pretty sure thing.

"Bryan—or whoever you are—you're standing right where I was told an enemy is supposed to be. Don't come any closer."

"I know, Mike. IT's just up ahead. You're being tricked! The thing waiting for you is going to destroy you and take your soul. This could be really bad. Please, you've got to believe me!"

But Mike was still wary. "What are you doing here?"

"They let me come here to stop you before it's too late. I'm here to warn you! I've been waiting here for a long time, Ace, knowing I could catch you when you got here. Anyone who goes farther down this road will be destroyed by the creature! So many have died down there. This place is evil. Please, you're being tricked!"

Mike was studying everything this boy told him. It sure seemed like it was Bryan—the boy looked and sounded just like Mike's best friend. Then Mike asked the boy questions about classmates and game stats—things only Bryan would know. They stood facing each other, and Bryan got the facts right.

Slowly, Mike began to relax. This boy knew all the right answers. Bryan really *was* there. No evil creature could have known what only Mike and Bryan knew. His intuition was still on full alert, but surely this was really Bryan!

But something weird was happening—the boy was starting to sweat. "Hey, Bryan, what's the matter with you?" Mike questioned.

"Ace, you're the greatest! But right now you're really back home in the hospital, pretty banged up from that car. Remember? You've been floating ever since—in a coma, and not quite yourself—evil beings could trick you." Bryan swept his hand around at the mountains. "All this is a fairyland. It's fake! Everything you've been shown and all the cute, colorful fairy houses are just bunk to fool you away from your soul!" Bryan's breathing was getting heavier and heavier.

Mike knew that Bryan wouldn't lie to him. But he also couldn't believe that the angels he'd grown so close to would try to steal his soul! Mike knew who he was and what he'd seen and experienced, yet Bryan sure sounded like he knew what he was talking about, too. And he had all the right answers!

"I can't stay much longer. This place is really bad, and I need to go back to a good place. We can't stay long in such bad places, can we, Ace?"

"That's what I hear."

"Well, come with me then. There's a heavenly opening under the tree over there. I can take you back with me. You can snap out of your coma back on Earth, and save your life and your soul.

Please come with me!" Bryan was getting weaker and weaker by the minute, and Mike thought he saw the boy's image start to blur.

Everything in Mike's body told him that this Bryan wasn't telling the truth—yet there was his trusted buddy, pleading with him to go back to his life on Earth. *What if this land is a fake?* Mike thought. *No. It can't be.* Mike's inner being knew it. But he wanted to be absolutely certain. *What was the name?* Mike remembered. He'd memorized it back at the Red House.

"Reeneuy!" It was the name for Bryan that Mike had learned at the red House of Relationships. Mike stared at Bryan, and Bryan stared back.

"What, Ace?"

"Reeneuy!" Mike slowly backed away.

"Is that some fairy word you learned here, Michael?" The boy was getting pretty nervous now. His clothes were getting wet with sweat.

Mike stood very still. Chills crept up the back of his spine. Bryan had never called him Michael. The armor on Mike's body began to vibrate. The shield on his back was beginning to move back and forth on its hook, as if it wanted off. Finally, Mike answered. "No. Reeneuy is your heavenly name, and you didn't know it."

The two just stared at each other for what seemed like hours, but was really only seconds. The game was up. The trick hadn't been good enough, and IT didn't have the energy to keep it up. IT was ready to fight.

"**ENOUGH!**" With a shout that was as loud as ten men, the figure that had been Bryan began to change shape. Slowly, the small, sweating boy changed into a huge, disgusting creature. Wide-eyed and ready, Mike moved back as IT grew to at least 15 feet tall. The beast's eyes shone red like volcano fires—its skin was warty and an ugly green, and it smelled like it hadn't washed in ages. The monster's hands were huge, with large, dirty finger-nails, and arms that were much too long for its body. Although its legs were short and stubby, Mike had already seen how fast they could move.

Mike backed even farther away from the hideous creature. The thing growing and changing before him grossed him out completely. IT wasn't human and wasn't a beast. IT was unnatural and didn't belong in any world that Mike had ever been in. The smell was unbelievable, and the face on the huge bald head kept changing from one horror to another. There were razor-sharp teeth in that mouth—when you could see it in the ugly mass of warts and skin. That big nose couldn't have worked, because its own smell would have been too much! Was IT real, or was this another trick? Mike didn't know.

IT showed Mike the shocking power of the old energy. IT was just the opposite of peace and love, and it smelled like death. The look on its face was full of hate, as if it were about to smash Mike like an ant. IT hated Mike so much and was determined to wipe him out.

Mike could barely stand to look at the thing, but then he realized that this was the way IT wanted him to feel. He snapped out of it and stood up straighter. *Not everything is as it seems,* he repeated to himself.

He suddenly realized that IT was showing off—making itself huge and terrible and gross to scare Mike more.

Mike's body was automatically ready for anything. The vibratory level of his new being was still on full alert. Like an old warrior who'd fought many battles, his body hummed with power and life—but Mike stood still. His sword began to sing quietly. Still, Mike did nothing. But he had an idea. Now it would be *his* turn to play a trick.

"You're so big!" Mike pretended to be afraid. He ducked and raised his arms up in front of him to cover his face, making his voice shake. "You're the real beast—here to take my soul?"

From behind folds of green warty skin, Mike heard the thing's real voice for the first time. **"So weak!"** IT said, thinking it was mightier than Mike. **"I knew it."** The deep and dangerous voice reminded Mike of something out of one of those old horror movies that were on TV late at night.

"Please! I'll do whatever you want," Mike squeaked. "Do you want me to go to the tree? To the door to heaven?" Mike's sword began to jump up and down in its sheath. He hoped the creature wouldn't hear it.

"Don't be ridiculous. I'm here to kill you." The thing was so confident that it grew bigger yet. Mike realized that IT could probably be as big as it wanted.

"Who are you?" Mike shrieked. He was doing a good job of pretending—the thing seemed to believe him completely. What an egomaniac that monster was!

"I'm the part of you, 'Ace,' that's the REAL Michael Thomas! The strong part! Take a look at your power! I'm the part of you that thinks, not feels. Trying to look like Bryan may have been a trick, but the words were true, boy. You are indeed in the hospital, in a coma, and I'm here to get you out of this pretend land of fairies and angels and bring you back to real life. To get you out of here, I have to destroy the foolish spirit you've become!"

Mike realized that a lot of what IT said was true. IT really was a part of Mike—an old, ugly part—a part he'd worked so hard to change here, a part that he wanted gone forever. He ducked a little lower and shook a little harder. *Don't overdo it,* said a voice inside.

"And you have to kill me?" Mike's sword was rattling like crazy now, ready to fight, but that just made IT think even more that Mike was shaking with fear.

"In a way, yes. Your death in this land of fools will wake you up and bring you back to the real world. I've watched your silliness since you first walked through the gate, and luckily I was able to slip in behind you. I've been trying to snap you out of it ever since." The thing was starting to move toward him.

"Am I that silly?" *Keep IT talking,* Mike thought. *Keep shaking, sword!* He sent his thoughts to his weapon. *It's a good distraction for the beast.*

"It was easier to believe the angels' baloney because you're so weak right now. Nothing here is real, boy. They've tricked you so well that I have to completely destroy this part of you to save your mind and your soul. I hate everything you've become!"

Mike had to act fast. "Before you kill me, can you prove what you're saying is real? If you are the thinking part of me, then help me figure this out!" Mike knew that this ugly thing wasn't going to wait much longer, but he thought he could buy a little more time if he pretended that IT had control.

"Of course I can." IT hated this land of make-believe and wanted to squash this fairyland forever. IT was the real world, where there were no pitiful weaklings like Michael Thomas. IT thought things out and was sensible, believing only those things that could be proven.

The creature stood up to its full height. "The one who is correct here has all the power. Only the mind knows the truth! That's why I can exist in this pitiful world—because I am Truth. Nothing here has power over me!" IT let out a roar that hurt Mike's ears and actually seemed to bend the grass down around Mike's feet, instantly turning it the same greenish brown of its horrible skin.

"Really?" Mike grinned at the beast. The trick was over now, and he stood up as tall as he could. "Then let the proof begin!"

Mike never knew he could move so fast. His balance was perfect, and he was swift as a rabbit. Thanks to what he'd learned from Orange, he found himself on a rock as tall as a man, closer to the monster! His sword jumped from its sheath and began to hum as soon as it found itself in Mike's hand. It was a strange sound, full of power and promise. Mike held the sword, not pointing it at the creature, but pointing it to the sky. In one lightning-fast motion, he pulled the shield off his back and held it up—its beautiful silver face pointed at the beast. Michael Thomas, the warrior, stood ready.

IT was totally shocked. IT had been sure that the battle was over—and that IT had won. But now what? Was the boy going to attack? *How foolish,* IT thought. IT would swat this little pipsqueak like a fly; it would almost be too easy.

Mike was so near that IT had to back up to use the long arms that hung down to its knees. IT drew back, clenching its powerful fingers into huge fists, ready to attack.

As the creature got into position, Mike's voice rang out: "BEHOLD THE SWORD OF TRUTH. LET IT DECIDE WHO HAS THE POWER."

As soon as Mike said this, the beast attacked. IT looked like a huge train—coming at him at top speed. The next moment, an unbelievably bright light flashed from the blade of Mike's sword and struck the beast with a mighty force. The blow didn't stop IT, but it did knock IT off balance. IT swung an arm at Mike. Mike automatically held his shield up to protect himself, certain that the mighty fist was going to smash him and the shield with a single blow.

But the shield and armor protected Michael Thomas. The armor instantly surrounded him with a bubble of protective light.

The shield shot little lightning bolts into the big, hairy arm. Light seemed to blaze up all around, flying in all directions! A strong, burning smell filled the air around them.

Instead of the crushing blow Mike expected from the creature's arm, Mike was filled with a feeling of lightness. The monstrous thing was instantly pushed back by the protective glow that surrounded Mike. The light was so powerful that it lifted IT off the ground and slammed IT backward, some distance away.

Mike wasn't hurt. He stood where he was, watching the beautiful light. He was in awe of the gifts he held in his hands! They'd worked perfectly together and had beaten back the giant. Mike noticed that the light that came from his weapons was pleasing to him, but IT yelled out in pain and covered its red, fiery eyes with a wart-covered hand. IT was used to the cloudy gray day, and couldn't see in all the bright light.

Mike smiled, realizing now that the weather was also a gift. He was calm and sure of himself as he spoke to the beast—he remembered something Orange had said. "Does the Shield of Knowledge bother you, my ugly green enemy? Darkness cannot live where there is knowledge. No secrets can live in the light, and there is light where there is truth!"

At these words, IT was up on its feet and charging Mike again, determined this time to wipe him out, once and for all.

Mike didn't know if he could stop the train again. An arm was one thing, but the force of the whole giant creature? He waited until the very last minute, then jumped off the rock just as IT came within inches of him. Again, Mike attacked, and again he surprised the creature—too close to catch, too tough to handle.

No fancy footwork was necessary—Mike just ran between the huge stubby legs. As he went through, he stuck his sword into the giant's underside. There were more flashes of lightning. Mike then swung his shield at one of the legs, and the slimy monster was slammed back again by a sudden burst of light. IT held itself and groaned as it flew through the air. Landing on the ground with a loud thud, IT rolled and roared in a smoking, wounded heap.

Sparks were still shooting from where Mike's sword had stabbed it. "That oughta do it!" Mike was cool, calm, and collected. He marched up to the creepy thing, with his sword held high, and stopped just beyond its reach. "Do you give up? Who has the truth here? Who has the power?"

"I'll die first!" croaked the pitiful creature in a little, tiny voice.

"And so it shall be." Michael Thomas was fearless, ignoring the smell from the beast that was getting worse and worse.

But the putrid creature was not through yet. IT was not a spiritual being. IT was, like Mike, a being with a body in this strange land of angels and lightning swords. IT hurt and IT bled.

Mike could see the terrible wound that the powerful sword had made and knew how much it had to hurt. A black fluid gushed from the cut, staining the ugly skin of the giant's legs. He thought IT had to be in too much pain to get up—but IT did!

IT was unsteady on its feet and could barely stand up. The light was so bright now that the monster's eyes were almost closed. Mike knew that he'd won.

Killing wasn't Mike's thing. He couldn't imagine ever killing anyone or anything on purpose. But he knew that killing here wasn't like killing back on Earth, and the creepy thing in front of him was not really going to die. IT would just lose the battle once and for all.

The battlefield was quite a scene. Mike's sword, shield, and armor still glowed with light. Sparks kept snapping and popping all over the beast's smoking body as it tried to stand up for a final attack.

Now the armor started to sing a song of victory. The light of truth, knowledge, and wisdom lit up the little scene in the narrow canyon of no escape, revealing the pitiful sight of a battered and beaten IT. It was like the story of David and Goliath. A small warrior of light fighting a huge creature of darkness, both warriors standing so close to each other, both refusing to give up. It was Mike who moved first again.

Mike was much quicker than the wounded monster. He attacked where he knew he could hurt IT the most, moving quickly before it could grab him. Mike let his lightning sword and shield do their work. Now the creature was in a panic, and IT swung its arms around to keep Mike away.

The wild, waving arms kept getting struck by the sword's lightning and pushed back by the shield. It was quite a sight. Not only was there an incredible light show, but the sounds were thrilling! The spiritual battle weapons sang loudly together. Orange hadn't told Mike that the weapons all sang!

The final fight was over in less than a minute. The sword and the shield beat the creature back. IT was lying on the ground. Every smelly green inch of IT was stretched out in front of Mike, shaking like some very rotten jelly. Blood gushed from all of its wounds, and it smelled so bad that Mike had to put his hand over his nose.

Suddenly, the sword, shield, and armor stopped singing, and the pile of IT started to disappear. **"I'm not gone, Michael Thomas. There will be another day,"** IT let out a loud groan.

"I know," Mike said, as he looked into the evil red eyes. Mike knew that even though IT was not really dying, the battle was very real, and he could have very easily lost. He could have been the one to fade away if his spiritual weapons hadn't helped him so much. He was glad the fight was over. The monster slowly began to disappear. Mike watched until only dust remained where IT had been.

Mike slowly put the Sword of Truth back in its sheath, but not before thanking it out loud. He did the same for his shield, and then strapped it back on. He hugged his armor and celebrated how well it had worked. Then the unthinkable happened!

Mike felt the three gifts getting lighter and lighter. They were disappearing as the monster had done. "NO! I need you! Please!" But Michael Thomas's weapons were blending into his body. "What now? Why are they leaving?"

"Michael Thomas of Pure Intent, you still have your wonderful gifts, but now you carry them inside!" It was Orange's soothing voice . . . the angel who'd given Mike the gifts in the first place. *"You defeated the giant and appreciated that your gifts helped you to do so. You earned the right for them to become a part of you, Michael Thomas, part of every cell of your body."*

Mike sat down on a nearby rock. "And the next battle . . . ?"

" . . . will be won the same way, Michael, but without an actual sword, shield, and armor. Truth lives in you now, as does the power of knowledge and wisdom. There is no beast that can ever take them away."

Mike thought about this, then called out to another angel. "Green, have I shifted again?"

"Yes, Michael. Now that you carry these gifts inside, you're complete. There's only one more of us for you to meet."

It was such a comfort to hear Green's voice again. "Who will it be?" Mike didn't want to wait until the next house to find out.

"The grandest angel of them all, Michael. You will see."

Mike stood up. "White, who was the beast, really?" He had to know, since he had a feeling that this answer would explain it all.

"It was the part of you without love, Michael. It was the human part that is always there and must always be dealt with. If not, humanity without love actually creates darkness."

White's voice was amazing, and it instantly comforted Mike. "Will IT come again, White?"

"As long as you are human, IT is behind you, ready to pounce. But love will keep IT weak!"

Mike thought about this. *Just one more lesson, then no more human body, no more IT.* He was eager to open the door to Home, the door to a peaceful, loving life with no worries—a life that would be spiritually meaningful.

Since defeating the beast, Mike had noticed that the gray clouds had parted, and the chilly breeze had given way to warm sunlight. He looked around the battle scene. There were the scorch marks where his powerful weapons had defeated the enemy. He touched his waist where his sword belt had been, then his chest where he'd worn the armor. He missed them, but knew that he now carried the power inside, making him a mighty warrior of love—just as Mary had been in the hospital. He smiled when he thought of her strength and thanked her for that vision.

Mike felt his chest again. He realized that the map and the pouch that had held it were gone, too! "The map!"

"It is inside of you, too, Michael." It was Blue again. *"Your intuition will be your map now."*

It didn't take long for Mike to walk out of the canyon. He found his way back to the blue sky and gentle rolling hills. He looked back and saw that there was a wonderful rainbow arching over the end of the canyon. It glowed brightly against the beautiful sky, marking the end of the canyon and the end of his journey. He walked ahead, staring at the magnificent rainbow, unable to take his eyes off of it.

As Mike got closer, he could see the source of the rainbow's light: Six angel friends on fire with color were there in the sky in front of him. They were so grand, so proud! Holding hands, they formed a rainbow of celebration for the human they called

Michael Thomas of Pure Intent. He passed under them, calling out their color names and thanking each one. Mike loved them so much—he felt a lump rise in his throat.

There was Blue, who'd shown him his map and the direction of his journey; Orange, giver of the wonderful gifts that had defeated the giant; Green, his comedian friend, who'd explained all about his body, stomped on his toe, and had given him the experience of his first shift in vibration; Violet, the motherly one, who'd shown him the lessons of his life, and how he was responsible for it all; Red, the terrible eater, who had marvelously introduced Mike to his spirit family; and finally, the loving White, so very pure and wise. White had comforted Mike after the car accident landed him in the hospital, and this same angel also helped him learn about real love by watching a pure woman of incredible strength.

Mike knew it was their way of celebrating his victory, for the next house was the last one, and he'd no longer need them in this land. His training was almost over. He'd learned well and passed a great test, beating the beast on his own. He knew that the angels were saying good-bye.

"I honor you, my friends!" Mike watched the glorious colors slowly disappear into the bright blue sky.

✳   ✳   ✳

It wasn't long before Mike saw the next house. The other houses had looked small from the road, but not this one. It appeared to be a gigantic brown mansion! As Mike came closer, he saw that it was not merely a brown mansion, but a *House of Gold!* Not just the color gold, but actually *made* of gold!

The lawn all around the building was huge, too, and very well kept. There were giant water fountains gurgling and splashing, and streams winding their way all around the grounds. The greens of the grasses and plants looked even more beautiful against all the flowers of unbelievable colors. The path ended at the entrance to the house. But this wasn't just any house, it was also a doorway—an entrance into heaven itself. The door to Home!

Mike was a bit nervous as he turned from the main road and walked up the long, winding footpath to the door of the great golden palace. Finally, he came to the large decorated door made completely of gold. It looked so heavy that he didn't know how he'd ever open it. He stooped down and took off his shoes, putting them in their spot. He knew he'd never see them again. Then he waited.

No angel came.

He wondered if it was okay to try to open the huge door himself and step inside—maybe like White, this angel couldn't go outside either. Mike pulled on the great golden door. It easily swung open as he pulled!

He stepped inside and couldn't believe what he saw. Everything was gold! The walls, pillars, and floors. The furniture and decorations. And there was that smell again—flowers! The smell of a thousand flowers filled him with a wonderful feeling of love. What an amazing, sacred place.

But while the other houses had looked small on the outside but were huge on the inside, this one was huge on the outside and smaller on the inside. And it wasn't arranged like the other houses were. All the doors and hallways here led to just one place. No choices to go this way or that—only one direction to go. The path through the house was amazing and beautiful and grand—but simple. No side rooms, no bedroom or dining room for Mike.

Mike was trying to figure out what he was feeling as he slowly walked through the hallways to wherever they were taking him.

Yes. This place felt like a church, a very holy place.

No angel had shown up yet, and Mike didn't know what would happen next—it was the only time he'd ever come into a house and wandered around without being greeted. After all the excitement of his great battle, Mike should have been hungry, but he wasn't. He was too excited.

Mike walked along the hallway until he came upon a door that looked unusual. It had a name carved on it. The writing was the same strange writing he saw back at the blue House of Maps, then again in Violet's charts. He knew that it must be the name of this house's golden angel, wherever it was. Mike opened the door and went in.

What an unforgettable moment. Michael Thomas stood in what looked like a grand cathedral, with wonderful stained-glass windows all along the walls. As the outside light passed through each glorious window, it spilled in rainbows on the golden floor like pools of waving color. The huge room was round, and he could see that the door he'd just come through was the only way into this room. A golden fog gently swirled around the room. As the fog floated through the rainbow pools of light, it caused little lightning flashes of bright color. Mike had to remind himself to breathe.

Slowly, he realized that everything about the house was made to honor what was in the center of this great room. There were grand staircases all around the room, but they only led up to balconies high over the center of the room. Mike studied the center of the grand chamber. It was heavy with the golden fog, but he could tell that there was something else there as well. Mike started forward—to the end of his journey.

It took Mike much longer than it should have to walk to the center of the golden fog. The holy place was much larger than he'd thought. Finally, he was only a few feet away from the center. He stopped. *What's in there? Something is there inside the fog, but what is it?*

Mike was almost at the center when an unbelievable burst of energy hit him and brought him to his knees! He kept his eyes down out of respect. His body was starting to shake with an incredible vibration that felt like it came straight from God's heart.

Mike knew that he was close to the door to heaven—and Home? But he didn't see an angel yet. Maybe there was no angel. Yet all the other angels had told him that he was about to meet the grandest of them all. Mike felt that there was an awesome being here, the holy and miraculous presence of God! He was still having a hard time breathing.

Mike raised his head and saw that the fog was clearing out. He stayed on his knees but straightened up to see what was happening. A large golden block slowly appeared through the clearing fog. Soon he could see steps cut into it, leading upward. *Is the door to Home at the top of those stairs?* The energy was getting very intense, and Mike felt very small. No matter what he'd been through in this land, he didn't feel like he was important enough to be in such a holy place. He was at the door to heaven itself and felt like a rag doll. The power of Spirit and the glory of God were so strong that he couldn't move. Just a few steps away was something far more powerful than anything Mike had ever imagined.

Mike kept his head up. He just had to see it. What magnificent angel could bring this energy? He hoped the intense vibration wouldn't be too much for him, and he could live long enough to meet this great being. Even if he were to be vaporized in the next few minutes, he had to see it!

Mike remembered the stories of what had happened to those who touched Moses' Ark of the Covenant. They'd vanished in a burst of vapor because they'd touched God. This could happen to him, too, if the energy he was feeling now got any stronger. His cells felt as if they were going to explode. All of them were trying to celebrate at the same time! Then he had the feeling that his heart was getting bigger. Mike was starting to be afraid—not that he was going to die, but that he wouldn't get to see the being that belonged in this last unbelievable house. The fog continued to clear.

The great golden block with stairs became clearer. It looked like a king's throne! Richly decorated, bright beyond words, solid as a rock, and as gold as anything could be, it seemed to glow with its own holiness. The angel must be sitting on it.

Mike burst into tears! He couldn't help it—his body was exploding inside with the grandness of this holy energy, and he felt waves of thankfulness and love pour from his heart. He just could not stop crying. The energy was thick, and he knew that the golden angel he was expecting to see was indeed coming down the steps. This was probably the actual guardian of the doorway to Home, the one he'd wanted to meet for so long— the one who knew everything!

Mike was a basket case; he didn't want the angel to see him like this. He wanted to be strong, but he couldn't even stand up! He wanted the Golden One to know that he'd passed the tests and killed the giant, but he couldn't even talk. *Who is this coming toward me with such power? What being in the Universe could stand for the force of God in such a powerful way?*

"Fear not, Michael Thomas of Pure Intent. You have been expected," said the great angel whose body could barely be seen as it came down the stairs. The voice—so quiet and peaceful— Mike had heard that voice before! This was little help . . . he was so full of love for this being that he still couldn't speak. As the angel got closer, Mike put his hand over his heart so it wouldn't explode right out of his body. Everything was getting blurry.

The magnificent angel floated down the glittering, gold steps, slowly coming closer to Michael Thomas—who was kneeling, shaking, and speechless. Mike still managed to wonder why the angel needed stairs.

The great, glowing body appeared first, the head of the Golden One still above the golden fog. Mike saw that the angel was huge, bigger than all the others he'd met. The golden color of its robes was so bright that it seemed to be electric. He could see the bottom of its wings now . . . he knew there would be wings! They vibrated like 10,000 butterflies, but without a sound.

This energy was more than he could take. But just then, the angel paused, and Mike realized that something was happening to him. He was being given a gift, and he knew it. A bubble of soft, white light soon formed around him, helping him to feel peaceful.

Mike breathed a sigh of relief and began to calm down. He was growing stronger. The angel had created a place for him inside this bubble of light where his vibration could exist next to such a Godly one.

Finally, he spoke, but he didn't get up. "Thank you, Great Golden Angel." He took a deep breath. "I'm not afraid."

"I know exactly what you are feeling, Michael, and indeed you are not afraid."

Mike tried to figure out the voice. It had the same kind of peaceful energy that White's voice had. It was big, filling the whole space around him, but quiet at the same time. And he'd heard it before, but where? He got up the courage to ask. "Do I know you, Great Holy One?"

"Oh, yes," came the wonderful voice. "We know each other well."

Mike wanted to ask the angel how they knew each other, but just couldn't. He had to remember his manners in this place. It was better to sit and be spoken to in this energy, and Mike honored the angel's greater vibration.

"Our entire time in this house, Michael Thomas, will last no more than a few minutes. Our visit means a lot to you, and you will learn a great deal from it. Our vibrations are so different that we can only be here together for a short time—but it will be long enough."

Long enough for what? Mike thought.

The angel went on, and Mike's body soaked in the music of that wonderful voice. "Michael Thomas of Pure Intent, do you love God?"

Mike's cells buzzed with action. That question again! Chills of realization raced up his back. He thought White was the last one who had to ask this, but he was wrong. *This is it!* His cells were all trying to talk again at the same time. *Tell him YES!* they begged. Maybe his answer to the Golden One would be his ticket through the door Home. He wanted his answer to be the best he could give.

But all he could think about was what an honor it was to be here with the magnificent golden angel, so the great momentous answer was just a simple, "Yes, I do." His voice was honest and pure. It didn't shake.

"And Michael Thomas of Pure Intent," the wonderful voice continued from the invisible face in the dancing golden fog, "do you wish to see the face of God? The one you say you love?"

Mike was very still. *What in the world does this mean? What's going to happen next?* Again his cells insisted that Mike say yes. He answered without thinking, "Yes, I do." His voice shook this time, and he knew the angel had heard it.

"Then, Michael Thomas of Pure Intent," said the angel as he moved down the stairs, "look at the face of God, the one you have told us that you loved—eight times."

The grandest angel of them all came even closer. Even inside his protective bubble, Mike felt the energy get much stronger. The angel was so huge that part of the fog still clung to him as he came down the stairs. Finally, he stood in front of Mike, the fog slowly clearing from his face. "Get up, Michael. You must stand for this."

Mike got up on shaky legs and searched through the last bit of fog for a glimpse of the angel's face. Michael Thomas of Pure Intent—the little human who'd seen just about everything on his tough road, who'd faced the giant beast and beat it, who'd made his changes better than any other human before him— shook even more on his shaky human legs at what he saw next. It was unbelievable; it didn't make a bit of sense to him. He sank to his knees for the second time in this great golden house.

The face of the great spiritual being that had just come down the beautiful golden stairs from the huge golden throne was *the face of Michael Thomas!* This was no trick. It belonged to the angel. It WAS the angel. The angel was Michael himself!

"So, since you love God, you love me." The angel went on. "Time for another gift, Michael." The angel's voice was sending peace and understanding deep into Mike. "I give you the gift of greater understanding, Michael, as you listen to me explain."

With the angel's gift, Mike's mind started to clear. The angel spoke again.

"There is something inside each human that fights against believing that humans are truly a spark of God, Michael." The angel smiled.

For Mike to look at him, it was like he was looking into a mirror, smiling at himself. It was so weird. The angel's voice was *his* voice, but he hadn't recognized it. He needed to hear what the angel was saying, and now his mind was clearing to allow for it.

"I AM your higher self, Michael Thomas, the part of God that lives in you as you walk on Earth. This is your last lesson before you reach your final goal. This is the last information you have to truly understand before you can go on. It is the most important truth for all humans—the truth that usually stays hidden and is the hardest to believe."

Mike knew how important it was to pay attention to the angel's words, but it was hard to watch him speak because he had Mike's face! Still, Mike had to go forward. He had to know more.

The angel moved a bit and floated to one side, and Mike could see more of the golden carved stairway. "This is the golden House of Self-Worth, Michael. Nothing will stop you faster on your journey of lessons than the feeling that you haven't earned your place here. So, we decided to tell you who you really are. You are part of me, Michael. We humans are the grandest angels of them all. We are the ones who have chosen to go to Earth, learn all the hard lessons of human life, and make Earth's vibration higher as we learn those lessons. We are the ones who make the difference for all humans, as well as the whole Universe. Believe me, Michael Thomas, what you did on Earth made great changes in other places."

"But I didn't stay!" Mike blurted out what was on his mind, hearing what the angel said but still feeling that he'd given up too soon. "And I didn't learn anything while I was there!"

"It does not matter, Michael. At least you chose to make the journey, and your agreement to go through it all is honored greatly. Did you not know this? You have heard the story of the prodigal son in Sunday school."

Mike remembered the story but hadn't applied it to this situation. The son in the story didn't want to do what his father wanted him to, so he ran away from home. He came home after living life his own way, and his father welcomed him home with love and a huge feast anyway. The father knew the son had to make his own choices in life, and he honored those choices.

The angel moved again as it went on with the explanation. "Michael, the other angels loved you so much! Did you not wonder what you had done to deserve such a wonderful honor? Now you know. We—you and I—are a special group of much loved and honored beings who have chosen to come to Earth, to live in a body of lower vibration, unable to remember how loved and honored we truly are. YOU are actually a piece of God, walking the earth to learn all of your lessons so that you can bring more light into the world. And you are seeing your higher self, that piece of God, in front of you now."

Mike was really impressed. He thought back over the past few weeks in the angel houses. The contracts he'd learned about in Violet's house were amazing. The family he saw and met in Red's house filled him with wonder. But now, what an idea that he, the little human Michael Thomas, was actually among the highest angels of all! And the other humans, too! *Could I really be so grand?*

"Yes, you are, Michael. Yes, WE are! It is time now that you understand and realize that you deserved to come to Earth. You planned to come, and you actually stood in line! You are honored for what you have done, and you are worthy now to go on to the next step. You have said so many times during your journey that you love God, SO YOU MUST ALSO LOVE YOURSELF! Think about this, Michael Thomas, for the truth of it will change how you think about your path and what you will do."

Thanks to the Golden One's gift of understanding, Mike was able to understand all that his higher self explained. This was truly hard information to accept, though. He just wasn't used to thinking of himself as so wonderful.

"The last step now—and it would have been the last step even if you had stayed on Earth—will be to accept your wonderfulness. Know that it is real! Feel how loved and honored you are to be a human. *Feel that you belong here and are forever!*"

Mike had a flashback of his time with White, seeing Mary in the hospital. Now he understood what White had meant when he said that Mary had accepted the Golden One! That's what he was being asked to do now. "Did Mary know about you?"

"Mary knew about her own higher self, Michael, if that's what you mean. She worked together with her higher self the whole time you watched her. She knew who she was. She knew about the golden room and the golden throne. She knew she was sacred and that she deserved to be on the Earth. She *owned* her sacredness."

Again, Michael was very impressed by Mary, this small woman who'd shown him so much, and he'd never even known her.

"Oh, she knows you, Michael."

"She does? How?"

"Just as all of us know each other. She fully understood that her gift to her father that day was having a great effect on others. Her intuition told her so. She even knew she was being watched. As you do now, she had all the gifts and tools and maps inside her, and also the golden gift of understanding that I am passing to you. Such is the power of the enlightened human on Earth."

"Wow." Mike was learning so much, and he had so much more respect for Mary now. She *knew!*

"The test is next, Michael Thomas."

Mike swallowed hard. The angel was getting right down to business. He knew that there'd have to be some kind of test. *How would this great angel with my face and my soul know if the human Michael Thomas was ready to own his sacredness?*

"There is only one way." The angel floated off to one side. "Don't be afraid, Michael, but I must take back your gift of the protective bubble for the rest of our time together. Either you have understood and accepted the truth, or you have not. This test may not seem hard, but there is no way to pass it unless you are pure and have accepted the truth of our being partners."

Mike was worried. The protective bubble was disappearing, and once again he felt how intense the Golden Angel's God-force vibration was. All that love. This time, though, he felt something new. He felt a little tingle of being part of it all. *Was this the test?*

"I feel it!" Michael called out, hoping that this was it. Would the test, whatever it was, be over now? No such luck. Instead, the angel with Michael Thomas's face came toward him.

"Michael Thomas of Pure Intent, sit down on the third step."

Mike was starting to have trouble breathing again. His cells simply had a hard time handling such high vibrations. He had to get control over his body—and right now! "*We* are okay," he said to his cells. "Don't be afraid! *We* have earned this. *We* are good enough for this!"

Mike was shouting and he knew it. He was automatically doing what Green had taught him, and it was working. He sat down on the third step of the great golden throne and soon he was calm again. Mike suddenly realized that the Golden One was watching him closely. He saw the biggest smile on that golden face!

"You really do know what to do, my little human partner. These are things I could not tell you, but you have learned them well from the others. Now let us see if you have learned my lessons as well."

The next thing that happened shocked Mike even more than seeing that the angel had his face! The grandest angel of them all was beginning to kneel. The golden wings spread all the way out like a huge, magnificent fan as the angel bent down toward the floor. Mike's body reacted again, but it didn't make his legs weak and drop him to his knees this time. Instead, he almost exploded with love as he watched what the angel was going to do.

As he knelt, the grand angel took out a golden bowl and held it gently in front of him. He looked right at Mike and spoke loving words to him. "This bowl is a symbol of all my tears of joy for *you,* Michael Thomas. With this, I wish to bless and wash your feet, for you are great and deserve this honor."

Oh no! This Godly being is going to actually touch me! Now Mike understood the test. A touch from this golden one would show whether Mike's cells had really understood how wonderful they were and if his body truly knew how holy it was. No wonder the test couldn't be faked. This was it!

The angel paused before he touched Mike's left foot and answered the questions in Mike's mind. "It is not a test of change in vibration, Michael. For you and I'll never be the same vibration until we join together again at the end. This is a test of your human belief. WE must absolutely believe that WE, as God, deserve to be human. How you handle having your feet washed by Spirit lets all of us know if you truly love yourself as much as you love God."

Mike relaxed. He knew his own mind and knew that he'd learned this lesson from the Grand One and accepted it. The angel would see that, too. He was ready. The huge angel knelt just below Mike's eye level to honor him. Mike saw this honor and felt himself fill up with even more love.

The Golden One gently took Mike's foot, and an unbelievable tingling feeling went up Mike's body—right up into his very heart and mind. He was starting to overflow with love, and the tears just rolled down his face. He said nothing as the angel gently washed his foot. Mike felt that he was loved beyond measure. He didn't disappear in a puff of smoke. He could feel the intense energy between them, and was barely handling it, but felt that he was worthy to receive it.

Mike stayed quiet, because he knew love was quiet. He knew that since love has no expectations, the Glorious Golden One wasn't going to ask him for anything in return. He knew that love didn't brag and puff itself up, and that the angel wasn't going to suddenly be joined by the rest of his angel co-workers. This was just between Mike and him, and the angel was quietly asking him to accept the honor and just BE. Mike couldn't describe the feelings he was having. He cried tears of great joy and thanks, but he wasn't ashamed to cry. He knew that the angel understood that this was a human's way of saying thank you—strange as it might seem.

Finally, the angel spoke again. His voice was full of pride for Michael. "Michael Thomas of Pure Intent, you have indeed passed this great test—one of the greatest of all. But now I'll show you something even greater. Even though you have passed all the tests, and even though you are ready to walk through the door to Home itself, I'll now wash your other foot. It is my honor to do so, and shows the love that God has for you. The test is over. I do it only because I love you. Don't ever forget this moment."

There couldn't have been a more holy moment in Mike's little human life. He couldn't stop crying, and love continued to be shared by two beings of the same soul force as the golden angel gently washed Mike's other foot.

Finally, it was over. The bowl disappeared, and the angel stood up to his full height, his wings folding again behind him. "You may get up now, Michael Thomas. Your intent has been shown to be pure indeed, and you are ready to go Home!"

Mike got up, looked around the huge room, and then back at the angel.

Knowing his thoughts, the angel took Mike's hand and pointed to something behind Mike. "Up the stairs, Michael." The angel smiled again.

Mike turned and looked up into the swirling golden fog. The steps on the golden throne would lead him to yet another unknown place of great purpose. He looked back at the angel to make sure he was supposed to climb the stairs by himself.

"The door you are looking for is there, Michael. Oh, yes, and remember this: *Things are not always as they seem.*"

Mike didn't stop to ask about that since he was already so used to hearing it here.

The angel gently moved next to Mike, putting his huge arm around Mike's shoulder. In that soft, comforting voice, the angel spoke his last words: "I just came from there myself, Michael. It is okay. You have to go now. I'll join you there soon . . . we never say good-bye, since we are of the same soul force."

Mike knew he had to leave this strong energy. He turned and quickly started up the steps. Now he understood why there were stairs. It was for the human, not the angel, and the steps were spaced apart perfectly for Mike's foot size. It was time to graduate! Time to go Home. He stopped one more time to look back at the Golden One, the piece of God that was he, smiling like a king at Michael Thomas from the bottom of the stairs. The angel was right. There was no feeling here of good-bye. The angel really was part of him!

Mike began to realize that within the last several hours he'd met two parts of himself: the one without love, and the one with it. It was his choice to decide which one to be.

Thick fog still hid the top of the stairs, and Mike could only see about ten of the golden stairs at a time. He climbed slowly—

he hadn't come this far just to fall off this tower at the most important part of his journey! He laughed at the thought of tumbling to the ground and then having to apologize to his grand higher self for being so clumsy. The little laugh helped him to relax.

Now Mike could see some kind of landing just ahead. *What a magnificent throne! It's really huge, and it's mine!* Next to a giant, beautifully carved golden chair, was the door he'd planned on seeing for these many weeks. It seemed to be hanging in midair, with no walls around it. It wasn't part of the house he'd just left, or part of the throne either—it was a doorway to somewhere else and seemed to have a different vibration. There was much writing on the door, most of which he couldn't understand, but in plain English was the word *HOME.*

Mike had waited a long time for this. He couldn't believe how much he'd grown up in this angel land. He stood there thinking again about having his feet washed by the angel, the most important and loving thing that had ever happened to him. He faced the door with a little ceremony.

"I earned this!" Mike was quite sure of himself. "And I honor the Universe for letting me choose to do what I'm about to do. With complete love, I go through the door to where I have asked and hoped to be." He took one last deep breath of human air and bravely opened the door marked *HOME.*

✳   ✳   ✳

Then Mike threw up.

✳   ✳   ✳   ✳   ✳   ✳

Chapter Twelve

Through
the Door to Home

"Hold his head to the left, next to the tray!" cried the nurse to the orderly. "He's vomiting."

The emergency room was crowded that night, as it was almost every Friday night. There was a full moon, too, which usually made things worse. Most people think it's just an old folk tale that the full moon has a strong effect on us, causing more accidents and crazy situations than at other times. But just the same, many hospitals make sure that there are plenty of doctors and nurses in the emergency room on those nights.

The nurse looked down at her beeping pager and rushed out of the room to take care of another sick person.

"Is he awake?" asked Mike's mom.

The white-coated orderly bent down to take a closer look into Mike's eyes. "Yes, he's coming out of it. But don't let him get up—he's pretty banged up, and he's going to be very sore for some time."

The orderly left the room, closing the curtain so that Mike and his mom were alone again. The emergency room was noisy all around them. Lots of people, lots of pain. Many of them had been there almost as long as Mike had—about an hour and a half.

Mike opened his eyes. He knew immediately where he was . . . back on Earth in the hospital where his journey had begun. The lights were so bright that he had to close his eyes again. It was cold in the room, and Mike cried out for a blanket. His mom got up from her chair just as the orderly came back in the room with one, as if he'd heard Mike out in the hall. Then he left again.

"You've been out for a while, honey," said his Mom. "They had to put some stitches in your head. Don't try to talk." She patted his hand and went out into the hall to find the doctor. She wanted to know how soon she could get Mike home and in his own bed.

Mike's head was swimming. This had all been a dream! It was just like IT had told him . . . he'd been on Earth the whole time, lying in a coma in the hospital. He felt like he was going to throw up again, this time because he was so depressed. He was back . . . but not Home.

Home *was* just a dream, and the land of angels was exactly what the monster had said it was—fairy talk. All that he'd seen and learned was fake. He closed his eyes and wished he could die.

"Michael Thomas, are you awake?"

"Yes," said a very tired and very sad Mike.

"You can go now. We stitched up your cut and you're fine. It's okay for your mother to take you home now." Mike opened his eyes and saw a friendly nurse with a clipboard smiling down on him.

"But what about my stomach—my legs?" Mike wondered if he would need a wheelchair, or some crutches.

"Nothing's wrong with them, Michael. Did we miss something?"

Mike felt his stomach, and it wasn't sore. And his legs weren't burning anymore. Everything seemed to be okay now. He was very puzzled. "No . . . I guess I just dreamed it."

Then Mike's thoughts turned to school—he must have missed a lot of days. He hoped he wouldn't be too far behind. "Excuse me, nurse, how long have I been here?"

"A couple of hours, Michael." The nurse winked at Mike and began to fill out some paperwork on her clipboard.

"Is that the bill? I don't know if my mom and dad have enough money for all this."

The nurse smiled and said, "Don't worry, Michael. All of this will be taken care of by the man whose car hit you. His insurance will pay these bills. Your parents won't have to pay for a thing."

"Thank you, ma'am."

The nurse finished her paperwork and left Mike alone again. *This just doesn't make any sense,* thought Mike. It seemed like the accident must have happened months ago, and Mike remembered very well how sore his stomach was and how badly his legs were hurt when the car hit him. And strangest of all, Mike had been home from the hospital for a week before he'd left on his journey through the gate in the row of bushes. So it couldn't be that it was just a dream—*could it?*

Mike suddenly had to go to the bathroom. And he had to go right now! This was the real deal all right—he was no longer in the land of the angels.

Mike got up, ignoring the ache in his head. He realized as he looked around for the bathroom that he was still in his school clothes. Mike spotted himself in the mirror. His face looked different. He got closer and looked into his own eyes for a long time, wondering what the difference could be. He was standing up straight and felt good! But he was hit by a *car*, for heaven's sakes! Well, maybe the two-hour rest in the hospital was exactly what Mike had needed.

A few minutes later, Mike's mom came back in to take him back to the house. He was so glad to see her and gave her a big hug.

His mom just smiled and said, "You've been through a lot, honey. Let's go home."

Mike was very depressed at hearing the word *home,* and he felt a stabbing pain in the pit of his stomach. His dream was just another puff of smoke. This was not the home he was hoping to go to.

"Sounds good, Mom." If he couldn't be in heaven like he'd hoped, then Mike was very glad to be with his mom. During the car ride, he asked her all about what had happened. Mike was sure he remembered—but he wondered how his legs could have been hurt so badly in the accident only to be in perfect working order a few hours later. Was it just his imagination?

When they got home, his mom tucked him into his bed so he could get some more rest. The smell of a late supper came floating down the hall from the kitchen, but Mike wasn't hungry. That food couldn't be half as good as the angel food he was now used to eating. In the dim light of his room, he could see that his brother's clothes and trash were still all over the room, just like when he left that morning for school. He felt even more trapped now. He just didn't want to be here anymore. *I thought I was going Home!*

Mike realized that he was not the same Michael Thomas he had been. He thought back over all the things that he'd done in the angel land. He felt like he belonged there. *But that was just a wonderful dream.* Then he fell into a deep sleep.

✳   ✳   ✳

Mike opened his eyes as soon as he heard his mom's voice calling out from the kitchen for him and his brother to get up and get dressed for school. He had gone to sleep sad and confused, but when he woke up, he felt wonderful. He felt peaceful! He knew that today was going be an absolutely great day, and he could hardly wait to get to school.

Then it happened. He stepped on a stray baseball card on his way out of his room and it made him think of Bryan again. But it didn't make him sad. It didn't make him want to just disappear. Mike actually made a face when he thought about how he'd acted before all this happened. *Ugh! What in the world was I thinking? Bryan and I planned all this, and that's just how it is.*

Next, Mike did something that he hadn't done in a long time. He ran to the bus stop and talked to all the kids waiting there. When the bus came, he jumped on it and sat down right next to somebody new—a kid in his grade named Joey who'd just moved to the neighborhood. They joked and laughed all the way to school. No one knew what to think about this. They were all used to the quiet and sad Mike. Who was this kid?

By lunchtime, Mike was really amazed by how much he'd changed. He was doing things that weren't like his old self. He felt the energy of the moment and didn't worry about school or the team, or even about how messed up his room was thanks to his brother.

He knew that he'd make other friends. He knew he'd get back on the team. He knew that there was no changing his brother's sloppy habits. None of this worried him anymore. This was not like the old Mike. This was a new Mike who understood how good he was and how things worked in the Universe. He was starting to feel like he'd been born all over again. He felt chills go up his spine and knew what they meant. Mike was happy with himself.

He took his lunch outside and sat at a table close to the huge old oak tree. *Man, I bet I could see everything from the top of that tree!* Mike thought as he stared up into the branches. Then someone tapped him on the shoulder and asked, "Can I sit here?"

Mike jumped a little—he had already started thinking about the cool fort he could build in a tree like that. "Oh, hey Joey. Sure, you can sit here. Isn't this just the greatest tree you ever saw in your life?"

Joey smiled and sat down with his lunch. "It's pretty great. You should have seen the tree house I built with my friend at my old house."

Joey and Mike settled in like they'd known each other forever and talked about everything. Mike was excited to find out that Joey loved to play baseball, too. Mike even found himself telling Joey about what had happened to him on his journey. Joey thought that was pretty cool. Before they knew it, it was time to go back to class.

Joey felt really good around Mike—having a friend made him feel less nervous about starting out at a new school. He was sure things were going to be all right here after all. Mike was full of energy and didn't seem to let anything bother him. Joey decided he was going to try to be just like Mike and felt that he'd just found himself a good friend.

They said good-bye and went back to class. The rest of the day passed, and Mike went home with a peaceful feeling in his heart.

After supper, Mike sat in his room trying to do his homework, but he just kept wishing his dream was real. If it was, then why was he back on Earth? Nothing seemed to be working out as Mike expected it to. *Not everything is as it seems, I guess.*

Mike was starting to feel a strange but familiar presence. His intuition was giving him a nudge, and his body was speaking to him. He scooted his chair away from his desk, past a wad of dirty socks and a worn-out soccer ball, toward the middle of the room. There, he did something that felt absolutely normal to him, just like it had back in the angel land. He closed his eyes, held out his hands, and spoke out loud in a little ceremony:

"In the name of Spirit, I ask that I be shown what I need to know next. I celebrate it, even though I don't understand it."

Mike then sat quietly with his eyes closed. Suddenly, everything exploded in a burst of bright light.

Mike whooshed from his room to a place beyond this world that was made for him and for him only. It was the special inner place where Mike could speak with Spirit, where he could take time out to think about things. *This isn't really a dream, is it?* Mike thought as he floated out of his chair and into the new space.

"No, it is not, Michael Thomas." Mike was sure he'd just heard the voice of White—but he was afraid to open his eyes. He thought that if he did, he might find that he was just back in his room. He didn't want to go back to his room until he was good and ready.

"Is this real?" Mike asked.

"It is just another state of being. What feels real to you now, Michael?"

"White!"

"Yes, Michael."

"It's so good to hear you!" Mike was very excited. He almost shouted. "White! It wasn't a dream! I knew it!"

"It was not a dream, Michael," the angel answered.

"What happened? Why didn't I go to heaven? Was there a mistake?" Mike was so happy to be talking again with his spiritual friend!

"Open your eyes, Michael. We have company."

Mike opened his eyes slowly. He was still in this wonderful place, still floating in the unbelievable whiteness.

Below Mike were seven colorful shapes moving around in a big circle. He watched as they slowly changed. Each one was a misty cloud of color, slowly getting bigger and taking shape. He knew what was happening, and his heart jumped with joy!

The seven clouds got brighter and brighter—Blue, Orange, Green, Violet, Red, White, and even GOLD! The small clouds became the huge angels Mike had met and spent time with—it seemed like it was only yesterday. Mike was overjoyed to see them. His friends were here!

The seven angels stayed for a while, hands raised upward toward Mike in ceremony. He celebrated with them. He felt an unbelievable holiness around the circle, and honored it by not speaking. It was the Golden One who spoke first.

"Michael Thomas of Pure Intent, we greet you!"

"And I greet you!" said a thankful and peaceful Mike.

"What is it that you wish to know, Michael?" The Golden One was almost laughing. He knew that Mike was dying to know the answer to the question: *Why am I here on Earth again?*

It was White who spoke next, in answer to Mike's thoughts.

"Maybe you would like to go back over what you actually asked for, Michael." Mike didn't know what White meant, but he was quiet while the great angel continued. Like a tape recording, Mike was suddenly hearing a playback of what he'd said at the beginning of his journey, when he was talking with White about what he felt Home was.

I want to be loved and to be around love. I don't want to be so sad and lonely anymore. I want to know that every-thing will turn out all right, and that I'll be able to do what

I'm supposed to do in my life. . . . I want to be like you. That's what going Home means to me.

It was quiet for a moment, and then Blue spoke. "Look at your life, Michael Thomas. Your intuition is the map that will lead you to a peaceful life, since you understand how Spirit works in the here-and-now."

Mike realized that Blue was right. He wasn't worried about tomorrow. He had his "map," and it would lead him to the place that was right for him.

The voice of the orange angel came next. "The gifts and tools of your high vibration give you the power to kill any negative thing that should ever try to get in your way!"

Mike knew that Orange was telling the truth. He wasn't worried at all about the troubles of the past. Bryan was gone, but Mike knew that was part of the plan and that he would make new friends . . . maybe Joey.

Then came Green's voice. As always, it was filled with great laughter. "Your body will take you wherever you need to go in your life, Michael. It's now filled with wisdom and knowledge."

Mike had never felt better, and he knew now how to stay in great shape thanks to Green!

Now it was Violet's turn. Her voice was soft and silky and floated to Mike's ears. "You're now part of God's plan, Michael, with purpose and responsibility. You make your own life, so you never need to worry again. The family is always around you!"

Mike knew she was right. He'd make his own future, without worrying about it in the meantime. He knew his family would always be there to help him, and he'd always be in the right place at the right time.

Red's voice spoke up. "You'll never be the same human you used to be, Michael. You've been changed forever by your own intent."

Right again! Mike could never go backwards. He was not the same kid—he was new!

Then White's spectacular voice sounded again. "You are an honored part of love's plan, Michael. You are loved without measure, and you have the power to give the same love to others. You have yet to realize the gift before you."

Why is White always the one whose answers make me have more questions? Mike thought, smiling to himself.

And finally, after all the other angels had spoken, the voice of the Golden One rang out. It was so large and powerful, so sacred, yet soft and gentle. "You wanted to be like an angel, Michael. What is it you learned in my house? That you are a wonderful part of God, walking the planet in a very high vibration. You are an angel in disguise—and one of the few humans to know it. You have been chosen by God."

Suddenly, the angels spoke as one: *"This IS Home, Michael Thomas. You are here because you asked to be here. It is where you belong, and where you can best help the whole planet. Each thing you asked for is now in place. You are a Warrior of the Light. You ring out with the vibration of God. You have killed the giant, accepted the Golden One, and have the wisdom of the ages!"*

There was more, and Michael Thomas knew it was coming. The angels faded back to colorful clouds, and seven small clouds of bright color blended together into one huge cloud of bright light like a diamond! The sparkle of that cloud was unbelievable! The angels were having a meeting. Mike's intuition told him so. After a few minutes, he heard them again speak as one.

"Michael Thomas, we give you a new name today. As you walked the road, you were known as Michael Thomas of Pure Intent. You stand here today as a graduate, a being with high vibrations who is not quite a human, but not quite an angel. Instead, you are now Michael the Current. *Your new name shows that you have*

made the long journey. You have learned to be in the vibration of the Now, and this is one of the best compliments we could give you."

Mike knew that the angels were serious in their honoring of his new vibration. The brilliant diamond cloud slowly changed to the actual shape of a diamond and seemed to rise up from below and flow over him, taking up the whole space he was in with its diamond light. He felt the love wash over him, and again was awed by the presence of God. The feeling went through every cell of his body, then he knew it was time to go back to the chair in his room.

The angels had one more message, though, and as Mike floated back to his chair, the words of their blending energies rang in his ears: *"Michael the Current, YOU ARE DEARLY LOVED."* Then, the great swooshing feeling that had carried Mike to the white place swept him home again. He felt himself gently settle right in the middle of his own room.

Mike sat for some time in his chair after this wonderful visit with his angel friends. Everything that had happened to him on the path and in the angel houses was real! Everything the angels had taught him was true, and all the knowledge and power was still his as he sat back home in his room. Mike's head was spinning with these thoughts, and he wondered how many other lucky people like him were out there.

Mike was very tired and still had homework to do. He barely got it all done! He finally made it to bed, too tired to think about what would come next. He had to sleep, and he did—like a rock!

Mike was ready for school the next day. He looked out over the schoolyard from his seat on the bus and thought he could do anything he put his mind to. He would indeed make a difference wherever he walked. He knew that there was still a lot to learn and work out—especially how to be "Michael the Current" at the same time that he was Michael the little human around others. But Mike wasn't worried. The angels all loved him so much, and because he had the gift of understanding from the Golden One inside of him, he'd always be able to handle any situation.

School was easier to deal with than Mike had thought it would be. He did all his homework, and his grades improved. His teachers and classmates noticed the new Mike and were glad of it. He signed up for baseball again, and was playing center field in no time. Joey even agreed to be Mike's locker partner next fall in junior high.

A few weeks passed. As Mike lay in bed one night listening to his brother's snoring, he remembered something White had said. He'd been so busy in his new life that he'd almost forgotten! *Michael, you have yet to realize the gift before you!* His eyes filled with tears as he realized what White was talking about. The greatest gift of all—one that would only come to him if he were still human. The thought of it made him shake all the way down to his toes. He'd grow up and be a man after all! There was a chance for him to find Anolee later! Mike's heart pounded as he thought about the cool life ahead of him.

* * *

Here is where we leave Michael Thomas. He has a quest. Because of his new intuition, tools, and gifts, he knows that he won't be complete until he grows up and finally meets Anolee. His intuition will guide him in the right direction, and the Sword of Truth inside of him will be his light in the darkness. Mike has a clear picture in his mind from the White House that he'll never forget.

Nothing will stop Michael the Current from making the most of his life and finding the sacred gift that is waiting for him somewhere out in the world. It's just a matter of time. His smile is as big as that of any person who is on a quest such as his. And he knows he's going to make it.

When Mike grows older, he'll look for the beautiful red-haired woman with skin like ivory and eyes like emeralds. He doesn't know her Earth name, but it doesn't matter. The energy of Anolee will be like a lighthouse in the darkness to his soul. The thought of the family he'll have with her will make him a stronger person.

The angels smile and know, too, that Michael will find her.

Michael Thomas is indeed *Home*.

*   *   *   *   *   *

About the Author

Theresa Corley is a grandmother, writer, artist, musician, and energy worker. She recently retired from a career in business, which lasted 26 years. She welcomes hearing from each and every one of you! Please feel free to contact her by e-mail at: **tcorley210@aol.com.**

* * *

From Theresa, on how she came to write this adaptation:

I've been interested in studying different spiritual paths for many years now. I've enjoyed reading books by many lightworkers, including Edgar Cayce, Paul Twitchell, and Kryon (channelled by Lee Carroll). But I worked in the corporate world until I received the call to my *real* life in 1997.

During the winter holiday season of 1997, I first saw the movie *The Night of the Iguana*. I bought the video and watched it umpteen times. Each time I saw Ava Gardner in beautiful Mismaloya, Mexico—which is a village only a short hop south from Puerto Vallarta—my heart ached with a mysterious homesickness. Then in January 1998, during my reading of Kryon Book Six *(Partnering with God: Practical Information for the New Millennium),* it became explicitly clear to me that I was to actually go to Mexico to free the angel inside. I bought a guidebook, and looked daily at the beautiful pictures of the waterfront.

Crazy as it may seem, I traveled to Puerto Vallarta that April with a friend, knowing that the reason would later show itself. We walked all around the old town, eventually finding in the blinding sunlight Richard Burton's house and the house he bought for Elizabeth Taylor as he filmed *Iguana*. In between our little treks, we rested in our cool room at the Hotel Yasmin, reading *The Journey Home*—I'd already read it, but I read it again—my travel partner read it, too. A few times during that reading, I wished to myself that someone would adapt the book for children. And each time, I got the strong impression that I should just do it myself. Toward the end of our stay, the Yasmin staff happened to repaint the ironwork chairs and tables in the lush inner garden—starting with the two chairs we always sat in to discuss *Journey*. They painted them *gold!* The color of the last angel we meet in *Journey*—our higher self! And on our last morning there, I woke up out of a vivid dream hearing: "*Señora . . . abre la puerta,*" ("open the door").

Things got back to normal when we returned home, and I put off the adaptation, feeling that that was a job for someone better equipped. It was my higher self that kept reminding me that I had the tools, and that I was to use them. Finally, I forced myself to give in to Spirit.

On June 12, 2000, I wrote a letter to Lee Carroll, author of the original *The Journey Home*. I explained that I felt it necessary to adapt his wonderful book so that children might also enjoy it and learn its lessons of love, encouragement, and support. His reply was equally loving, encouraging, and supportive. I haven't looked back since.

— Theresa